Welcome to the January 2009 collection of Harlequin Presents!

This month be sure to catch the second installment of Lynne Graham's trilogy VIRGIN BRIDES, ARROGANT HUSBANDS with her new book, *The Ruthless Magnate's Virgin Mistress.* Jessica goes from office cleaner to the billionaire boss's mistress in Sharon Kendrick's *Bought for the Sicilian Billionaire's Bed,* and sexual attraction simmers uncontrollably when Tara has to face the ruthless count in *Count Maxime's Virgin* by Susan Stephens. You'll be whisked off to the Mediterranean in Michelle Reid's *The Greek's Forced Bride,* and in Jennie Lucas's *Italian Prince, Wedlocked Wife,* innocent Lucy tries to resist the seductive ways of Prince Maximo. A ruthless tycoon will stop at nothing to bed his convenient wife in Anne McAllister's *Antonides' Forbidden Wife,* and friends become lovers when playboy Alex Richardson needs a bride in Kate Hardy's *Hotly Bedded, Conveniently Wedded.* Plus, in Trish Wylie's *Claimed by the Rogue Billionaire,* attraction reaches the boiling point between Gabe and Ash, but can either of them forget the past?

We'd love to hear what you think about Presents. E-mail us at Presents@hmb.co.uk or join in the discussions at www.iheartpresents.com and www.sensationalromance.blogspot.com, where you'll also find more information about books and authors!

EXCLUSIVELY HIS

Back in his bed—and he's better than ever!

Whether you shared his bed for one night or five years, certain men are impossible to forget! He might be your ex, but when you're back in his bed, the passion is not just hot, it's scorching!

That's how it is for the couples in this brand-new miniseries from Harlequin Presents. He really is better than ever, at least in the bedroom. Last time it didn't work out. This time everything is different. But hold on tight—in these stories, it's going to be an emotional, passionate, heart-stopping ride!

Look out for more EXCLUSIVELY HIS novels from Harlequin Presents in 2009!

Trish Wylie

CLAIMED BY THE ROGUE BILLIONAIRE

HARLEQUIN®

TORONTO • NEW YORK • LONDON
AMSTERDAM • PARIS • SYDNEY • HAMBURG
STOCKHOLM • ATHENS • TOKYO • MILAN • MADRID
PRAGUE • WARSAW • BUDAPEST • AUCKLAND

ISBN-13: 978-0-373-12794-8
ISBN-10:   0-373-12794-4

CLAIMED BY THE ROGUE BILLIONAIRE

First North American Publication 2009.

www.eHarlequin.com

Printed in U.S.A.

All about the author...
Trish Wylie

TRISH WYLIE tried various careers before getting the one she'd wanted since her late teens. She flicked her blond hair over her shoulder while playing the promotions game, patted her manicured hands on the backs of musicians while working in the music business, smiled sweetly at awkward customers during the retail nightmare known as the run-up to Christmas, and has gotten completely lost in her car in every single town in Ireland while working as a sales rep. And it took all that character-building and a healthy sense of humor to get her dream job—which lets her spend her days in reindeer slippers, with her hair in whatever band she can find to keep it out of the way and makeup as vague and distant a memory as manicured nails. She's happy she gets to create the kind of dream man she'd still like to believe is out there somewhere. If it turns out he is, she promises she'll let you know...after she's been out for a new wardrobe, a manicure and a makeover....

For Cathy, who taught me about Alphas,
and for the Gabe "appreciation society"—
you know who you are!

CHAPTER ONE

SHE was back. And Ashling Fitzgerald hadn't changed a bit in eight years, had she?

Gabriel Burke had known exactly where she was since she'd made her grand entrance to her parents' equally grand party—just late enough to be 'fashionable'—dressed in a pale pink sheath of a dress that lovingly skimmed the curves and flat planes of her now near perfect body. He'd felt the hair on the back of his neck tingle, his eyes had found her in a matter of seconds and he'd watched with hooded eyes from the periphery of the large room as she worked the crowd with a smile constantly in place, her eyes shining as bright as the jewels sparkling around her neck.

Oh, she was *something* all right.

More polished than he remembered, maybe. But he'd lay odds she was just as much trouble underneath that newly acquired sophistication as she'd been before.

'Well, you certainly scrub up well in a tux.'

Gabe smiled as her brother Alex joined him in the doorway. 'Don't you have a girlfriend somewhere you need to persuade that you're a funny guy?'

'She's chatting to her favourite rock star.'

From his advantageous height Gabe could see Merrow

across the room, laughing at something the older man was saying. 'You wanna be careful there—she looks like she's enjoying his company more than yours.'

'Nah.' Alex grinned. 'You met him when you quoted the hotel renovation; he's about forty years too old for her—and, anyway, I'm even better looking in a tux than you are. Why would she trade down?'

'You gotta work on that, y'know; it's sad you haven't outgrown all that shyness in your old age.'

Yes, because that one month made all the difference in the world when they were both thirty.

They surveyed the room in comfortable silence for a few minutes while Gabe forced himself not to look for Ash in the crowd again. What she got up to wasn't his problem any more; he didn't need to keep tabs on her.

Then Alex helped no end by asking, 'You seen Ash?'

'Talking to your cousin Richard.' And he'd known that a tad too quick, hadn't he?

'I meant since she got home.'

Course he did. Gabe pursed his mouth for a second; rolling the couple of olives he had left in his hand back and forth before he shrugged. 'Nope.'

'Looking well tonight, isn't she?'

Well wasn't the word Gabe would have used. *Hot* would have been more accurate if he'd chosen to be honest. Because that was how she looked to anyone who didn't know what lay beneath that beautiful exterior. Gabe knew. And she could be as hot as the face of the sun and he still wouldn't think she was worth the trouble she'd brought his way last time.

Didn't stop his gaze from straying across the room again as she lifted a fine-boned hand to tuck her sleek hair behind one ear, though, did it?

Alex continued, 'She's fired up about this gallery of hers.

You should tell her you're doing the renovation work on it—that'll get you both talking again.'

No hurry necessary with that one, Gabe felt, and he wouldn't even have taken on the damn job if it weren't for the fact Alex had asked him to as a personal favour. 'She'll find out soon enough.'

Alex nodded. 'I know you rarely take on the physical part of it these days. And just in case I haven't mentioned it already—I appreciate it. The family is keen to have her stay home this time so, the sooner the place is up and running, the better.'

Gabe shrugged again. 'Be a good chance to make sure I can still do the work. No good yelling at crews when they mess up if I haven't lifted a power tool in years.'

'The benefits of being the boss old pal.' Alex grinned as he patted his shoulder.

Some days it didn't feel like much of a benefit to Gabe, but he didn't say that to Alex, because Alex probably wouldn't get it. He'd always worked at what Gabe considered the 'clean end' of the business. An architect might get the satisfaction of seeing his visions come to life, but there was nothing quite like building something, literally, as far as Gabe was concerned. Childhood building blocks, only bigger, Alex would rib him—but meet and greet and make the deals just didn't have the same sense of satisfaction, Gabe would argue back. He was a hands-on kinda guy.

'Your parents are headed for your girlfriend.'

He chuckled as Alex disappeared, then settled back to watch the rich and famous interacting in their natural habitat—wondering how they all managed to look so at home in their fancy clothes with their glasses of expensive bubbly while he still had a deep-seated urge to loosen his bow-tie, dump his jacket over the back of the nearest chair and go find a bottle of beer. A reflection of his background, he supposed.

Still, at least while he stood on the periphery he didn't have to make small talk; that was something.

But the peace and quiet didn't last long. The hair at the back of his neck tingled in warning first, his spine automatically stiffening when a familiar melodic voice sounded right beside him in tones that somehow went straight from his ears to his groin.

'I thought I saw Alex with you.'

'You did.'

'Do you know where he went?'

He could hear what almost sounded like an edge of nervousness in Ash's voice, and a single glance from the corner of his eye confirmed it. She couldn't look him in the eye, could she? Score one to the home team, then.

Turning, he leaned against the door frame, folding his arms across his chest. 'And I'm s'posed to keep an eye on *all* the Fitzgerald children now, am I?'

Her hazel eyes narrowed a little when she glanced up at him. 'Picking up where we left off, are we?'

'I'm just not as easily fooled by this new version of you as the rest of the room appears to be, that's all…' he leaned his face closer to hers, his voice lowering '…but then I know you better, don't I?'

She faltered for a second before clamping her lips together and glancing around the room. Then she stepped in closer, the scent of her expensive perfume teasing his nostrils as she lowered her voice the way he had, looking up at him from beneath long lashes.

'You know the old me. But I'm not going to argue with you about it in the middle of my parents' party so maybe we should just discuss the weather for now?'

'It's Ireland—it's been raining.'

He watched as the corners of her moist lips quirked, 'O-kay—that was a short conversation. So what do you want to try next—the economy? Politics? I'm open to suggestion…'

'Picking a topic kinda suggests I *want* to make small talk, doesn't it?'

She cocked her head to one side, a curl of dark blonde hair bobbing against the tip of one breast. 'Still hate these parties, then, I take it?'

'Depends who I get to talk to at them.'

'Yes—I missed you too, Gabe.'

He pushed off the door frame. 'Have you met Alex's new girlfriend yet?'

She extricated her elbow when he attempted to guide her into the crowd. 'You don't need to make introductions for me. I've struggled my way through enough of these over the years to know how to behave.'

'Ah, but the last social events I saw you at were ones I was rescuing you from before the gards arrived, so I wouldn't know how you manage at a grown-up party, would I?'

Ash sighed at his side. 'Can I just remind you that your superhero tendencies in those days were *voluntary*? I never asked you to—'

She stopped to chat to a couple of women who greeted her with the air kisses that always bugged the holy hell out of Gabe. But after eavesdropping on the words 'wonderful' and 'fabulous' at least a half-dozen times each, he'd had enough. And having seen Alex steer his parents away from Merrow, he saw an opening. So he wrapped his long fingers around her elbow again, smiling inwardly with an almost petty sense of satisfaction when she jumped in reaction, before he leaned in with one of his most charming smiles to inform the others, 'I just need to steal Ash for a bit.'

One step and she had her elbow free with another twisting

movement, robbing his fingertips of the heat warming them from baby-soft skin.

'You don't need to take on the role of escort for me—seriously, I can manage.'

'Merrow's on her own—so try being nice for once. Your brother will thank you for it. Consider it an attempt to prove you've actually grown up enough to consider other people.'

Ash sighed again, deeper this time, and Gabe tried to ignore how it lifted her perfect breasts against the deep 'v' of her halter neck or how her nipples were two distinct beads against the soft material. But of the very many things he was, he wasn't either blind or any kind of a eunuch—the sight garnering a very basic male response in him, which he wasn't the least bit pleased about, damn her.

But then the fact he'd noticed her 'attributes' once they'd hit puberty had been half his problem, hadn't it?

'Auburn-haired girl in the gorgeous dress, right?' Ash stated.

'How in hell would I know? It's a *dress*.' And noticing one dress entirely too much as it was, not to mention everything beneath it, had translated into an irritated tone in his voice and he knew it. So he took a calming breath before adding, 'But if it helps—yes, she has auburn hair.'

Ash stopped dead in her tracks, her eyes checking around them before she scowled. 'So are you planning on either glaring at me from across the room or shadowing me like some kind of chaperon all night long?'

He leaned down to answer closer to her ear, his eyes on the crowd so he wouldn't look down the front of her dress. 'Depends. Are you planning on getting into some trouble I should know about so I can be prepared to smuggle you out of here for old times' sake?'

When he leaned back Ash smiled briefly at someone she knew, and then turned her face towards him, her voice low.

'Look, I get that your memories of me aren't good ones, but can we at least try and—?'

'Be *friends*?'

And the disbelief must have shown on his face judging by the reply he got after she searched his eyes. 'We can't avoid meeting up at things like this, so maybe we should try t—'

'Didn't anyone tell you men and women can't just be friends, Ash?'

'You actually *believe* that?'

'I know from experience. So unless you're suggesting making up with me *another* way…'

The colour on her cheeks deepened as she lifted her chin an inch before turning away, and Gabe smiled a larger smile at her back. Because having the upper hand on Ash wasn't a bad feeling, especially when she'd run rings round him for so many years. And she wasn't messing around with a boy dependent on the approval of her family any more, was she? He'd paid his debts.

So if she wanted to try messing with him again she might find herself in a little deeper over her pretty little head than she planned for…

He watched the sway of her hips as she walked away, the floor length dress moving like silken liquid against her body, her long hair cascading down between her fine shoulder blades, curled ends bobbing as she swung round to greet her brother's girlfriend with a vivacious smile in place.

Yup, she was still the piece of work he remembered but she was also all-grown-up and then some. And normally a feisty, strong-willed woman wrapped up in as sexy a package would have encouraged him to play, wouldn't it? Add the temptation of a little 'payback' too and…well…

He got to Merrow's side in time to hear, 'I'm Ashling

Fitzgerald, Alex's sister. But you can call me Ash—everybody does.'

Leaning in towards Merrow on his way past, he muttered an addendum, 'When they're not calling her a pain in the ass.'

He then lifted one of the olives he'd been carrying in his palm, tossing it into his mouth before smirking smugly at Ash in the way he knew had always bugged her most as he walked by.

Ash waved one hand in dismissal while she shook Merrow's with the other, throwing out a retort just loud enough for him to hear. 'Pretend he doesn't exist. I've been doing it for years.'

So Gabe took a step backwards, whispering the words for her ears only. 'Except for that one time. Seems to me you knew fine well I existed when you were kissing me. And who knows what we might have done if your friends hadn't interrupted us?'

The flush reappeared on her cheeks as she turned to look up at him, her eyes narrowing in a way meant to warn him off, while Gabe's gaze purposefully dropped to her mouth as she whispered back, 'And we never will, will we? 'Cos even if we were the last two people left on God's green earth it's safe to say that'll never happen again—*ever*.'

She bit her teeth briefly against her bottom lip as she carefully enunciated the word 'ever', but one glance up into her eyes, where gold flecks in the hazel blazed at him in anger, Gabe found himself quietly laughing as he walked away. He couldn't help it, because, whether she'd meant to or not, she'd just laid down the gauntlet. The word *ever* suddenly was a challenge to him. He might just have to see about that...

Ash didn't get too far in forming a new friendship when her nemesis returned, forcing her to take a deep, calming breath as she caught the low undertones of his cologne when he appeared with a plate practically groaning under the weight of food from the buffet table.

'She recruiting you to her campaign of terror, then, Merrow? I hope you have a good solicitor.'

Oh, he could try goading her all he liked, but she wasn't getting into a full-blown argument with him when she was doing such a good job of working the room the way she'd been instructed to. So she nudged him hard enough in the stomach to make him lose an hors d'oeuvre to the floor.

'The only solicitor I'll need these days will be to get a restraining order to keep you away from me.'

Yes, when in danger fall back on the ways of old, Ash—that's a great way to demonstrate how much you've changed. Problem was it was just too damn easy to fall straight back into the role of Gabe's sparring partner when he was apparently so keen to believe she hadn't changed the least little bit. After all, what did he know about her now? She knew nothing about him—well, not beyond the fact that he'd grown up pretty well on the outside in the eight years since she'd left home with her tail between her legs.

He really had, hadn't he? The first time she'd caught sight of him across the crowded room her breath had even caught and she'd been unable to stop herself from stealing glances at him for the rest of the evening; not that he'd been hard to locate overseeing the crowd from the doorway, looking like the kind of guy who was poised to head off to a party way more fun and possibly one-on-one. Yes, the fact that he was in a tux helped, but she doubted if it would have made any difference if he'd been in jeans and a T-shirt. He just looked so, well, he was so damn—

'Ah-h-h, and the battle begins all over again.' Her brother slipped an arm around his girlfriend's waist, planting a kiss on her forehead before he attempted to steal food off Gabe's plate. 'You wouldn't think they hadn't seen each other in eight years, would you?'

Gabe held the plate out of his reach. 'Get your own, squirt. The buffet's that way.'

Ash couldn't help but smile at the interaction. After all, it was entirely more familiar, not to mention safer ground. And more like the better parts of the old times she remembered. But it did make it glaringly obvious that the relationships Gabriel Burke had with the Fitzgerald siblings were as different as night and day. Still, maybe if she *persevered*…

She quirked a brow at Gabe's plate. 'And there's actually food *left* for him at the buffet, is there?'

'I'm a growing boy.'

'You grow any bigger and the ceilings will need to be raised.'

A fact made all the more ridiculous by the height of the centuries-old panelled ceiling above them. But the man really was very tall—easily six feet three and even the cut of his tuxedo couldn't hide the fact that he was practically made of muscle. Add that to his mop of tousled dark hair, piercing blue eyes and the hint of a smile on the edges of his full mouth and, really, well, it was no wonder her breath had caught at the sight of him. It certainly explained why she was so flipping aware of his proximity, why her palms were suddenly clammy, why her pulse was beating a little stronger and why the room suddenly felt degrees warmer.

But then she also knew that part of that reaction could be laid squarely at the door of nervousness at facing him again. Because she couldn't really blame him for disliking her as much as he did, could she?

'Good things don't always come in small packages. Sometimes size *does* make a difference.'

Ash's gaze shot upwards to lock with his, where she searched for and found a devilish sparkle of meaning shimmering in bright sapphire blue. She even heard a burst of astonished laughter exit her mouth before she glanced at her brother and

Merrow to see if they'd heard him. But they were too wrapped up in each other to have noticed, so she shook her head.

'I can't believe you just said that out loud in polite company.'

'True, though. And I'm not in polite company, I'm talking to you,' Gabe answered.

'I thought it was size *doesn't* matter.'

He answered while still chewing. 'Nah, that's something women say to make their men feel better when they fall short of the mark…'

Ash gaped at him—and then had to look round again to see if anyone had seen her gaping. She'd been looking over her shoulder all damn night, constantly aware of how she was supposed to behave and the number of people waiting for her to trip up. But then as the one Fitzgerald who already had a history of 'tripping up' she really shouldn't have been as amused by Gabe's topic of 'polite party conversation' as she was, should she? She most definitely shouldn't have felt as if it was much more fun than the weather or the economy or politics…

She absolutely shouldn't be rising to the bait. 'Is it, indeed? And you'd know that because…?'

'Well, you'd probably know more about it than me—' he swallowed down his food and smiled a small smile at her before loading his fork again '—having dated the guys you dated when you were here last time. The last one over-compensated for falling short of the mark a little more than you'd planned on, though, didn't he?'

This time her jaw dropped further. 'Why, you—'

The tail-end of Merrow and Alex's conversation miraculously cut her short of calling him what she'd been about to call him for *that* little dig.

'Though I'm planning on forcing your sister to tell me *every* embarrassing story from your childhood, just so you know.'

Ash glanced at her brother in time to see him slap a palm against his chest. '*My* childhood? Good luck with that. I was the model child, I'll have you know.'

With a warning scowl at Gabe's smiling face, Ash turned away to focus on Merrow. 'Disgustingly, I'm afraid that's true.'

'You balanced him out.'

She ignored the droll comment. 'But I can show you lots of embarrassing pictures if that helps.'

Anything that would take her out of hitting distance of that inconsiderate great—

Here she was trying to be everything that'd been expected of her by her father on her return and he was right there trying to remind her of the constant disappointment she'd been to her family in the past. Yes, because she hadn't already spent the last few hours fending off knowing looks and thinly veiled comments on that past, had she? She hadn't had to smile her brightest smile and hold her head high while inside she wanted nothing more than to run off and change out of the expensive dress and jewels supplied for her into the worn jeans and comfy shirts she felt so much freer in.

And she definitely hadn't had to second-guess her decision to come home when France had been the first place she'd been allowed to be herself.

Gabriel Burke might have changed on the outside, but he was still the one person on the planet with an innate ability to rub her the wrong way. He'd just proved it in about five minutes flat. Well, no more. She wasn't getting sucked back into the same downward spiral of self-destruction. He could just take his brand-new disgustingly sexy good looks and his memory of an elephant and go straight to hell. She'd *tried* to be nice and make a little peace, but he'd just drawn a line in the sand again, hadn't he?

Like the day he'd changed their relationship for ever. When

he'd been twenty-one to her seventeen, they'd been to a party *exactly* like this and he'd found her outside kissing some boy she could barely remember now.

But she'd never forgotten what happened next...

CHAPTER TWO

THEY'D argued as Gabe dragged her across the lawn, Ash pro-
testing, 'I love him!'

'You don't even know what love is! You're seventeen, for
God's sake—what do you know about love?'

'He loves *me*!'

Gabe hauled her along behind him, his much larger hand
holding her smaller one tight. 'Love isn't what he's looking for,
Ash. Trust me.'

Ash dug her heels in, tripping over her own feet while he
ignored her and kept tugging her forwards. 'What would you
know? You don't even have a girlfriend.'

The next thing she knew she was slamming into his back.
She barely had time to catch her breath before he spun round
and she was off her feet being carried, Gabe's face a mass of
dark shadows inches from her own. And she'd never hated him
so much. Who was he to tell her who she could or couldn't go
out with? Never mind how much he'd just humiliated her by
tearing Miles off her and sending him running like a scared
rabbit, she was sick to death of being lectured.

It was *her life*! And he was ruining it!

'I don't have time for a girlfriend when I'm running around
keeping you outta trouble, do I? And some of us *work* for a
living.'

She could tell from the tone of his voice that he was angry, way beyond angry, in fact. When his voice went all deep like that with that tight edge to it he was *mad*. But she didn't care.

'Put me down.'

'No.'

'Yes.'

'No.' He stopped and turned, looking around him before marching over and sitting down on the old swing that hung from an ancient oak, plunking her across his lap. 'You need to understand this for your own good—that boy didn't bring you halfway down the goddamn garden to the *darkest* place he could find to declare his undying love. He came down here to see what he could get away with.'

'No, he loves me. I know he does.'

'And how exactly do you know when you've known him the equivalent of twenty minutes?' His arms formed two tight bands around her body to hold her still while she fought to get free. 'Because he *said so*?'

'Yes!' She struggled harder, her hands against his chest. 'You can tell when someone kisses you like that.'

Gabe had the gall to laugh. 'You can't tell if someone loves you from a kiss.'

'Of course you can.'

'No, you can't.'

'Yes—you *can*!' And that was when she made her first mistake. 'I bet you any money you can, 'cos if *you* kissed me I wouldn't feel *anything*.'

His arms tightened, hard, making it more difficult for her to breathe while she gripped fistfuls of his shirt to keep her balance as the swing moved. 'I bet whatever he made you feel I could make you feel and then some. Kissing and whatever else he had planned doesn't have to have anything to do with love.'

Mistake number two was: '*Prove it*, then. Go ahead and kiss me if you're so convinced—'

Gabe was kissing her.

It was the only thought she had before she got swallowed up in sensation. A whirlwind of sensation as she'd never experienced before. It was like—it was like—well—she had no idea what it was like.

And it was Gabe doing it to her!

She tried to lean back out of the kiss, but he lifted a hand, forcing his fingers deep into her hair before he adjusted the angle of his mouth on hers.

It was heaven.

His full mouth was warm, his lips firm, demanding, and Ash responded without thinking. Because it didn't feel as wrong as it should have, or that they were crossing a line, it just, it just felt good…

So, so good. And she wanted more.

When she ran the tip of her tongue experimentally over his bottom lip, he made a low growling noise in his chest. A warning? A protest? A 'don't stop' or a 'hell, yeah'? She didn't know. Had she done it wrong? This was just so different from when Miles had kissed her. She'd felt nothing resembling this when Miles had kissed her.

But when his fingers flexed tighter against her head and he deepened the kiss she got her answer. And when his tongue met hers and tangled, she felt something inside her shift and almost moaned aloud—immediately lifting her hand from his shirt to push her fingers into his short hair, urging him closer.

She wriggled on his lap to get closer, the swing rocked, Gabe steadied it with his feet, and then his other hand moved—sliding up over her knee, his fingertips skimming the soft material of her dress before confidently reaching below the long slit in her skirt to touch her skin and slide higher up her leg.

And Ash *did* moan then—she couldn't stop the sound from happening—because it was somehow too much and not enough at the same time. Having him touch her like that—

It made her pulse speed up oh-so-fast. It made her skin tingle. It made her breasts *ache*. And feeling her body respond in so many strange and unsettling ways should have made her want him to stop, shouldn't it? *Shouldn't it?*

Because it was *Gabe*!

She shouldn't want so badly for his hand to keep moving upwards; she shouldn't desperately feel the urge to widen her knees a little to make room for him.

Her head started to spin from the lack of oxygen her rampaging pulse was demanding, her nose was filled with his soap-fresh scent, a tight kind of knot thing had formed low in her abdomen and she didn't know—she didn't think she could— what was—

This was Gabe—*her Gabe*! How could he do all those things to her? Why was he doing this? Didn't he know she wouldn't be able to look him in the face ever again when he'd made her feel this way? *How could he?*

She heard the giggling first, and then, 'Oh, my God! That isn't Miles. Who *is* that?'

'Ash, what are you *doing*? Are you insane? That's your housekeeper's boy!'

It got really ugly after that.

'I should have just bought a goldfish.'

She muttered a list of less troublesome pet options as she jogged from room to room in search of Moggie—less rooms would have helped, mind you. But Moggie had been thrilled with the large house from the moment his paws left her too-small-for-the-both-of-them car after the *lo-ong* trip home to Dublin from Paris. And the expansive gardens that came with the seventeenth-century-mansion of her childhood days were his idea of paradise. The kind of paradise that ultimately brought on the need for the bath he'd just escaped from.

That was what she got for locking him up in a stable while the party was on the night before.

There was a loud crash, followed swiftly by several muffled curses. Oh, good. Now he'd killed someone, or at the very least crippled them. Ash sent a silent prayer upwards that whoever it was wouldn't attempt to sue his owner just because she had the Fitzgerald name.

She was already further in debt with her father than she'd wanted to be ever again.

Turning swiftly on her heel, she ran barefoot along the hall and then stopped dead, her eyes widening in surprise at the sight of Gabe flat on his back—his deep laughter echoing off the cavernous ceilings as he wrestled back and forth with a delighted Moggie.

And she was momentarily stunned into silence. It was the mesmerizing sound of his laughter that did it.

She couldn't honestly remember the last time she'd heard him laugh—at least not the way he was right that minute. And he really should laugh that way more often, she thought, with the oh-so-male rumble from deep in his chest echoing around the vast hallway. Should smile that way, with his blue eyes dancing and his full mouth open and curved so his stunningly straight teeth looked amazingly white in contrast to his tanned skin.

It reminded her of the Gabe she'd known when she'd been a kid. And the memory made her smile at him without thinking. But when he ruffled Moggie's woolly ears his gaze strayed upwards, locked with hers and in a heartbeat the light in his eyes died and his smile faded. Of course it did.

Ash rolled her eyes, taking a deep breath before waving the

towel held tight in her hand in Moggie's general direction. 'He got away from me.'

Gabe ruffled the dog's ears again. 'Who's a clever boy, then?'

'He discovered the compost heap in the garden and rolled in it, so he needed a bath before there was any chance of him being allowed back inside…' And why exactly was she making excuses? 'Well, he certainly seems to like *you*. No accounting for taste, I suppose.'

Gabe rolled over and sprang to his feet with surprising agility for a man his size, swiping his large palms down his jean-clad thighs to remove some of the water Moggie had covered him with.

'Animals and small children—what can I say?'

'Well, there's always an exception to every rule.'

His vivid blue eyes looked her over from head to toe in an irritatingly intense gaze, sending her pulse rate skipping erratically when he lingered for entirely too long on the part of her soaked shirt that clung against the outline of her bare breasts—her nipples tingling into peaks against the material, which just didn't make any damn sense.

People who didn't like other people did *not* have a physical response to them, unless it was a bad taste in the back of the mouth.

He then let his gaze slide down, over the knot she'd tied in her shirt to the bare skin at her waist, down further over the legs exposed by short cut-off jeans. And whichever part of her body he looked at felt as if she'd been physically touched, as if he'd actually put his hands there.

But as much as it bugged her that he'd just made her feel that way, she couldn't help but admit that there was a very basic hormonal reason for it; he just had a very male—well, he had a kind of edge—no, it wasn't that—he just looked so—

Damn him!

She folded her arms across her breasts, to hide her body's reaction as she tilted her head to one side, lifted an accusatory brow and glared at him.

Blue eyes sparkled in challenge, daring her to call him on what he obviously knew he'd just done, then he threw a half-smile down at Moggie, ruffling his ears before he turned round and began gathering up the chairs that had scattered when he was knocked over. And Ash should have just taken that as a good opportunity to grab Moggie and leave. But that would be running away, wouldn't it? Well, like hell.

She was done with running away.

Her bare foot tapped involuntarily on the tiled floor while she frowned at her dog as he followed Gabe back and forth with a look of complete adoration on his face. *Traitor.* Maybe there was a reason they weren't called 'woman's best friend'…

But she couldn't help her gaze following him either, could she? And standing there wondering what it was about Gabe that she just couldn't put her finger on was sad—very sad. It wasn't as if he was the first good-looking guy she'd ever set eyes on.

So what if he was so large it made her feel smaller than her own five feet eight—more feminine and fragile somehow while standing near to him? So what if she was suddenly fascinated by the size of his hands and how easily they'd be able to cup her full breasts—if he'd been the last man left on the planet, that was. So what if he really did move with an almost big-cat kind of grace—big deal. Big *fat* deal.

She shook her head and took a deep breath. He could be as sexy as he liked. And her traitorous body could react to his proximity as much as *it* liked, but it wasn't going to change anything.

He was still Gabe.

Unfolding her arms, she automatically lifted the chair

nearest to her, moving forward to add it to the stack and watching him glance at her from the corner of his eye.

Eventually, after another chair she felt the need to say something to fill the silence. 'Are there many more of these left inside?'

Gabe continued stacking, his deep voice flat-toned. 'Couple of loads. Why? You got a girl-guides badge to get for being helpful?'

'Many hands make light work—didn't anyone ever tell you that?' She lifted another chair, grumbling beneath her breath, 'And anything that gets you to leave faster has to be a good thing.'

She hadn't grumbled quietly enough. 'Careful now, Ash. You might make me think you don't love me any more.'

Okay, now he was starting to really annoy her. She slammed her chair down harder than necessary onto the growing stack. '*When* exactly did I love you?'

'Still have a selective memory, don't you?' He glanced briefly at her again, and then irritated her all the more by tutting at her. 'I remember a time when you called me "my Gabe"…'

'I was four—at that stage I still thought the tooth fairy existed. Granted, your magic wore off a little later than hers, but it still wore off.'

A large hand landed on top of hers when she reached for another chair, long fingers curling around hers, his heat warming her chilled skin. And then the air vibrated as his deep voice rumbled close to her bowed head, his breath moving a strand of hair that had worked loose from her pony-tail so it tickled the sensitive skin on her neck.

'Still enough magic left that one other time, though, wasn't there?'

Her heart thundered in her ears as he stepped a step closer, his voice lower, his fresh soap and hint of musk scent driving her insane enough to make her want badly to close her eyes and breathe a little deeper.

'Until you realized who it was you were kissing.'

Ash swallowed hard, twisting her hand out from beneath his. 'All right, that one I'm maybe gonna have to give you. I said things to you that night I should never have said. And I was wrong, okay?'

There was no denying it after all, and with maturity came the ability to admit your mistakes, right? Now if he would just leave first so she didn't have to 'run away', then she could get her heart rate to return to normal and have a long, serious talk with her body about the kind of male it apparently found so damn attractive on a cellular level.

Mind over body, that's all it is, she silently told herself, a few times in a row to make sure the message got through.

Gabe's eyes narrowed as she stepped away from him. Okay, this was a new ploy. Because she'd actually managed to sound as if she regretted it, as if she were—*sorry*? No, that wasn't right. And sure enough, when she'd managed to get a couple of feet between them, he watched her damp her lips with the tip of her tongue, take a breath, then she looked at him from beneath lowered lashes and he saw the fire come back into her eyes.

'But if that's your basis for hating me for all this time, it's a bit lame, don't you think? Kids can be cruel to each other, but we're both grown-ups now.'

Yup, that was more like it. And Gabe smiled at his moment of stupidity waggling a long finger at her as he stepped over her and set the chair on the stack. 'Oh, you're good. You almost had me there. For a second it sounded like you were apologizing. But then we both know the word sorry isn't in your vocabulary.'

'And it's in *yours*, is it?'

Gabe turned, pushing his hands deep into his pockets while he continued focussing intently on her face so he wouldn't give into the deep-seated urge to take a good long look down her body again.

'I've never had as many people to apologize to as you do.'

And there it was again—that brief hint of what looked like regret in her eyes. What kind of game was she playing with him this time? He watched the reaction time, almost counting down in his head how long it took her to come back at him. She pursed her lips, folding her arms again—which automatically drew his gaze back down to where the movement had created a more pronounced cleavage, white cotton rapidly drying with the warmth of her skin so he doubted he'd still be able to see the rosy tips of her breasts the way he had before through the wet material, even if she moved her arms.

She certainly projected a very different image from the one from the night before, he'd give her that. Gone was the veneer of sophistication and polished beauty and in its place a sexy-girl-next-door look—a very definite take-me-to-bed one, as it happened. With her hair in long curling strands around the face devoid of make-up and, if forced to voice an opinion under duress, all the prettier without it, he thought.

Then there was what she was wearing—or very nearly not wearing, dammit. Her cut-off jeans were so short they displayed an almost never-ending expanse of long, shapely leg, which naturally made his imagination immediately kick in with X-rated images of what legs like that would be like wrapped around him. Her shirt tied the way it was making the same sordid imagination think about pressing his mouth to the very feminine hint of a curve on her otherwise completely flat stomach.

Under normal circumstances he would've acted on how his body hardened by simply looking at her, but he knew Ashling

Fitzgerald too well to be swayed by rampant hormones. And in the few seconds it took him to remind himself of that she'd opened her mouth again and helped remind him some more.

'It's just as well your opinion doesn't matter to me, Gabe, or that one might have stung. It must be tough for you being such a saint amongst all us sinners.'

He was tempted to laugh at being named a saint, but if he laughed she'd have gained more ground than she already had by being so damn hot. 'Oh, I don't think I've ever claimed to be a saint. I've always known exactly who and what I am. And even if I didn't I had you to remind me, didn't I?'

'Like I have you to constantly remind me of what I was when I was too young and stupid to know what I was doing, you mean?'

'And you know better now, do you?'

Her chin rose with the defiance he remembered all too well from long ago. 'Even if I said yes to that you wouldn't believe me, so what's the point?'

'Actions speak louder, they say.'

She unfolded her arms and stepped closer, her eyes sparkling with anger. 'And you still get to be my judge and jury, do you?'

'Unless you can find someone else who's seen every side of you there is to see, maybe I do.'

'You arrogant son-of-a—'

'Now, now, Ash.' He leaned his upper body towards her, his dark brows rising. 'You don't want to start calling my mother names, do you? Not when she's one of the very few who actually *believes* you might have changed since you left…'

After a few seconds while she stood with her mouth open and her eyes wide, she lifted her hands and shoved him in the chest, hard. Not hard enough to move him back any, but enough to push him upright. And Gabe chuckled at how easy it still was to make her lose her temper, which earned him another shove.

'How in God's name someone as wonderful as your mother ended up with a son like you *astounds* me!'

'Wonderful, yes, but still just the housekeeper, right? Let's put things in perspective here.'

Ash shoved him again, harder this time, so he pulled his hands swiftly from his pockets and grasped hold of hers, pinning them against his chest. Then, with her smaller hands held secure, he leaned forwards, his voice low as he looked down at her parted lips and then deep into her flashing eyes.

'And I'm the housekeeper's son and should remember my place, wasn't that what you said?' He smiled and he knew damn well it was the kind of smile that wouldn't make it up into his eyes. 'You were the one who set the boundaries in this relationship, Ash. So as the housekeeper's son it's my role to see you as a spoilt little princess, isn't it? That means I've kinda gotta wonder what it is brought you home this time. What'd you do—burn your bridges in France same way you did here?'

She tugged on her hands, and when he didn't let go she searched his eyes with a frown and then he heard her breath catch.

'My God, you really do despise me, don't you? I mean—I knew that, but I don't think I realized just how much until now.'

Gabe continued to hold her hands, his gaze dropping briefly to where they rested on his chest before slowly rising to study the realization written all over her face. He could smell the suggestion of fresh flowers in her scent mixed with the hint of wet dog that clung to her shirt; he could feel the way the rise and fall of her breasts shifted the small amount of air between their bodies, he could see the brief flash of what looked like hurt cross her eyes before she blinked it away behind a mask of anger. And she almost managed to fool him again. Almost made him believe she might be different. *Almost*.

He forced the words out through tight lips. 'I'm way beyond that with you.'

'You'd rather believe I'm not worth caring about at all, right?'

He tilted his head from side to side, his eyes searching the intricate coving on the ceiling while his thumbs absent-mindedly brushed over the fine bones of her knuckles, dipping up and down. 'I'd say my days of wasting that much time even thinking about you are pretty much gone.'

Ash tugged on her hands again. 'And I'd erased you from my mind long before I left home so we both know exactly where we stand, don't we?'

He held on, gaze locking with hers. 'Ah, but that's just the thing, isn't it? 'Cos you're back now, and like you said—that means we can't avoid bumping into each other. The game begins anew.'

'Avoiding each other like the plague sounds like a much better plan to me.'

Gabe leaned in a little closer. 'Not gonna happen.'

She laughed in disbelief. 'Yes, it is.'

It was a sexually charged stand-off. He could feel it in every male fibre of his body and while she continued to look up at him with that defiant tilt of her chin and that challenge sparking in her eyes he'd never in his life been more tempted to kiss a woman into submission. To use his hands, mouth and body to bend her to his will so she knew exactly who was in charge this time around. It'd be angry sex if he let it go that far, he knew that; passionate and hotter than hell and even the thought of it had him hard. And it was tempting, oh, it was tempting. Maybe he'd even kiss her into submission and leave her hanging…

He angled his head, his gaze dropping to the lips parting to

draw in a short, sharp breath before she damped them again—
as if willing him to go right ahead and do exactly what he was
thinking about doing.

A wet nose nudged between them, accompanied by a plain-
tive whine, reminding Gabe of the real world outside his moment of insane fantasy. So he frowned hard and let go of her,
obeying the need to step back, as if that one step moved her onto
safer ground.

Then he ruffled the dog's woolly ears to reassure him as he
calmly informed her, 'Well, you might find that a bit tough
when your brother hired me to do the renovation on your gallery
thing. We get to do this every day for the foreseeable future.'

After a brief moment of charged silence, there was a splut-
tering sound from behind him while he turned to reach for
another chair.

'He hired *you*? You have got to be *kidding* me!'

CHAPTER THREE

'I WANT you to fire him. Get someone else—he can't be the only one with a building crew in the whole of Dublin.' Ash leaned her weight back on her heels to compensate for the weight Moggie was exerting on the other end of the lead.

Her brother sighed in her ear. 'You want someone else at this short notice then you'll pay a hellish lot more than he's charging you.'

'I don't care.' She pulled a face, because that wasn't true. She couldn't afford to pay above the odds. 'How much more is a hellish lot more exactly?'

Alex went silent for a brief moment. 'He's doing us a favour, Ash—he's a busy man.'

Wow, there were other lives he had to make miserable? This gallery was her dream, dammit! She'd thought about it for years, planned it for months, sank every penny she had into it and borrowed from her father to make up the deficit. And now she got to have Gabe stand over her, watching her every move and judging her?

Again?

And, more than that, she got to spend every day looking at him, watching his every move and *wondering*—wondering what in holy hell it was about him that had her so, well, so damn turned on, if she was going to be honest about it. Because she was; she'd even had the most erotic dream of her life the night after the chair incident in the hall. When he'd leaned his face so close to hers for several charged seconds that had seemed to go on for ever, his blue eyes darkening several shades before his thick lashes had lowered and he'd focussed on her mouth—and she'd lifted her chin that extra half-inch as if to silently say, Go ahead and kiss me, then.

Again!

Alex tried a different approach. 'Isn't it about time you buried the hatchet? He's a good guy, y'know.'

She snorted in disbelief, adjusting her mobile against her ear before she replied, 'Round you he maybe is—but you're the one Fitzgerald he actually *likes*.'

'It's not like you gave him much cause to like you before you left. You two would have argued over the weather, if I remember right.'

Ash sighed heavily, stopping in her tracks to let Moggie run rings round her—literally, his extendable lead tangling round her legs while she searched the hundred shades of green in the wild landscape beyond the immaculate gardens for words.

'I know.'

Well, there really wasn't much else she could say, was there? But maybe if he hadn't been so sanctimonious back in the day—

She could hear the smile in her brother's voice. 'Give him time, kiddo. He'll see you've changed. You needed some time to find who you were on your own and Gabe didn't see that happening. He only has the way you were before to go by. If you spend some time getting to know each other you'll end up friends like you were before—betcha.'

She waved a ball at Moggie to try and encourage him to run anticlockwise so she could get free. 'How much? 'Cos I could do with the money, you know…'

He laughed. 'Count to ten before you speak to him—that might help.'

'That's a lot of counting, Alex.'

More laughter. 'Try it.'

Oh, he had no idea how much counting it was going to take, did he? Because no matter how many times she told herself she could deal with Gabe—the simple truth was, she was struggling. Five minutes in his company was all it took to put her back up or force her to fight her body's responses or prod him into a reaction to *cover up* her body's responses. And when he did react he unerringly managed to either make her body respond all the more or hit on all the things that reminded her of how awful she'd been to him as a teenager. Which stung, it really did, even when she tried to tell herself it didn't.

Thing was, when you were as close as they'd once been you knew exactly how to hurt each other—and that was pretty much what she'd done when he'd confused the hell out of her by kissing her the way he had. She'd lost her childhood friend that day. And she'd hated him for a long, long time.

'Still there?'

Swallowing away a sudden tightness in her throat, she looked down at her feet and began shuffling anticlockwise, 'Yes.'

'Still want me to fire him?'

Oh, how much did she want to be able to say yes to that? But she couldn't, could she? She couldn't afford to pay above the odds. And she couldn't allow herself to do Gabe out of the job, dammit, much and all as she currently couldn't stand him—he was bound to have bills to pay too, as did his crew. And they'd been guaranteed the work and taken it in favour of another paying job.

By digging her heels out of childish spite she'd be doing

damage on a larger scale. And she couldn't, no matter how much a part of her *really* wanted to.

'No. Dammit.'

'That's the spirit. We Fitzgeralds don't quit that easy.'

'Yeah, well, maybe half the problem with *being* a Fitzgerald is we don't know *when* to quit.' She knew she was free when Moggie tugged her forwards again and she managed to follow without tripping. 'Now tell me about this list of places to live you've found for me to look at and then you can tell me all about Merrow. Should I be warning her about life as a Fitzgerald yet?'

'Don't you dare.'

'What are you doing here?'

Gabe looked at Ash with a blank expression. 'Baking a cake—what does it look like I'm doing?'

She watched as he threw a giant plank onto a pile by the rear doors without so much as grunting at the effort. And frowned all the harder as she felt a completely unwarranted physical reaction to the simple action. What was it with her and blatant maleness? She'd read plenty of stuff that explained the whole basic animal instinct of mating with the strongest of the species theory, but *c'mon*! This was just getting ridiculous. She'd never been made to feel she was so damn ready for sex that a physical need would override her common sense. *Ever.* Even in her worst days.

And she hated him for it.

So she took a deep breath, looking anywhere but at him. She just had to consider this day one, didn't she? She could do this.

She counted to ten. 'I didn't realize you'd be here to go over the plans with Alex, that's all.'

'I find it's a mite easier to build something if you know what it is you're building in the first place—' he shrugged wide shoulders '—but maybe that's just me.'

Ash gritted her teeth. But attempting to let some of his comments go instead of rising to the bait every single time would help as well, wouldn't it?

So, duly letting it slide like a good little girl, she braved a couple of steps further into the empty warehouse, a smile touching her lips as she allowed herself a moment to savour the thrill of being one step closer to her dream. She wasn't going to let Gabe's presence ruin it for her.

Okay, so it might not look like much yet, but with a little work, some imagination and a good dose of passion thrown in...well, it was already magical to her. She'd probably have thrown her arms out wide and given it a big hug if she hadn't been so completely aware of another presence nearby.

Sighing deeply in resignation, she glanced in his general direction—not at all surprised to find him staring back at her.

'Problem?'

'No.'

Ash nodded at the plank. 'Could we put down the weapon before approaching the enemy, do you think?'

With a shake of his head he tossed it over onto the pile. 'How can you look that pleased with this dump?'

'Maybe because I don't see it as a dump?'

'Newsflash for you: Currently it *is* a dump.' He rocked forwards onto the balls of his feet, dropping his chin to look at her with a sparkle of amusement in his eyes.

Ash took yet another deep breath—nope, she wasn't going to get into another argument any more than she was going to pay any attention to the slither of anticipation shivering up her spine when he kept walking towards her. She was going to prove she could behave like more of an adult than he could *and* that she was in total control of her own damn body.

'Well, when you and your guys have done the work I'm sure it'll be something amazing.'

'I had no idea you had such faith in my abilities.'

'I have faith in Alex's abilities—all you've gotta do is hit a nail in straight.' She counted to ten and tried again. 'I have every faith that you can bring Alex's visions to life if you hit enough of them.'

There, that was better.

Gabe circled her before standing facing her, studying her with hooded eyes until she honestly thought she'd strangle him if he didn't say something to take her focus off his breathing or the hint of his scent or the way a lock of dark hair was falling into his eyes.

'Trying to be nice to me is the latest plan, is it?'

She swallowed hard, folding her arms when the deep rumbling of his voice did things to her breasts, as if her overly sensitive nipples could feel the very vibration in the air. Then she lifted her chin to study him while she counted to ten yet again.

'And what would you do if I *was* nice, Gabe? Wouldn't leave you much room for being nasty in return without seeming childish, would it?'

He lifted a large hand and ruffled his mop of dark hair, leaning his head towards one wide shoulder and then the other as he continued studying her. 'Well, I guess it would depend on just how *nice* you were planning on being, really, wouldn't it?'

The words were out before she could stop them, 'Gimme your definition of "nice".'

Gabe closed the gap, towering over her so she had to lean her head back to look up at him, which gave her disobedient gaze an excuse to linger on his mouth before she caught herself on and looked into his eyes.

She couldn't help a burst of almost nervous laughter from escaping when she read the meaning there. 'Oh-h-h, I don't think so.'

Which was a tad at odds to every pore in her body yelling, 'Yes, yes, yes,' wasn't it?

'Didn't you ever hear the expression "kiss and make up", Ash?'

'And that's all it would take, is it?' She mulled that one over for a moment, 'Cos—you know—if it *helped*… But then look where kissing him had got her last time, and that was before he'd become this, this apparently intense, compelling, almost hypnotic—

Damn him.

'It might take a little more than that.'

'Like what, for instance?' She really didn't know when to quit, did she?

'I've been known to appreciate a woman with a little imagination and a spirit of adventure. The world knows you have the latter in spades so maybe we should just see how you do with the other one?'

Oh, he had no idea what her imagination could do. If for a single insane second she considered describing to him some of her nocturnal imagination's ways of 'making up with him' what would he do? she wondered. Ask for all the hot and sweaty details? Challenge her to a demonstration?

No, she knew exactly what he'd do. He'd gloat that she'd had them and she'd have to live with him knowing.

So she smiled sweetly. 'Go to hell, Gabe.'

He smirked, leaning back as he took a breath, expanding his already broad chest, 'You know what your biggest problem is gonna be here?'

'Apart from you, you mean?'

When she blinked lazily at him he leaned back down, his

deep voice lowering. 'You don't know what to do about me, that's your problem. 'Cos you're stuck with my company for the next while and you can't pretend to be someone you're not while I'm around.'

'You don't know *who* I am, you just *think* you do—' she smiled the kind of smile she hoped sincerely looked as dangerous as the one he'd worn earlier '—and that's your biggest problem here.'

She then watched dense dark lashes brush his skin as he blinked, she watched as he searched each of her eyes in turn, and his calmness forced her to purse her lips tightly together to stop herself from saying something to make things worse.

After all, they were at the opening end of weeks of forced proximity and they couldn't spend the whole time arguing, could they? She lifted her brows when a thought occurred to her.

And Gabe's mouth quirked at the edges in response. 'There's more, I take it?'

Placing her hands on her hips, she stood as tall as her heels would allow her. 'What you need to do is pretend you've never met me.'

'Do I, now?'

'Yes.' She nodded firmly, as if to disprove the fact that the idea hadn't just that second arrived in her head. 'And I'll do the same with you.'

'Really.'

'All right, then, you come up with a better suggestion for working together for a while.'

'How about…' he turned his profile to her while he thought, then back, leaning his face closer to hers, his warm breath washing over the end of her nose '…you stay away 'til the work is finished?'

'Not happening.'

'There's always the "be nice to me" option…'

'Not happening either.'

'Scared you might enjoy being nice to me?' He smiled an even more dangerous smile—one that made her breath catch and her disobedient body tingle from head to toe. 'Until your friends interrupted us I seem to remember you enjoying being nice to me well enough. I remember the noises you were making, the way you clung to me, the fact that it wouldn't have taken much for me to move my hand higher…'

Ash hated that she had to swallow hard and take a breath before she could speak, visions of her night-time fantasies suddenly playing across her frontal lobe causing her tone to be clipped. 'We might need to just remind ourselves who it was kissed who that one time, don't you think?'

'Only if we remember who goaded who into doing the kissing.' His darkening eyes lowered to study her mouth the way they had in the hallway that last day, as if just talking about kissing made it something highly likely in the next few minutes.

She should so not want it to happen as much as she did, staring up at him with wide eyes, her pulse skipping erratically in her veins as she ran her tongue over her dry lips. 'If we do that then we'd need to look at what we were doing before the whole kissing idea was brought up.'

His gaze swept to a point above her head, his brow creasing into a frown beneath what were now several thick waves of dark hair. 'Hmm, you might be right…' And then his gaze locked with hers again, his voice a husky grumble that vibrated the heavy air between them. 'Now what *was it* we were doing? Refresh my memory…'

Ash's heart thudded up painfully against her chest as the answer hit her. Arguing—that was what had started the chain reaction last time, wasn't it?

Gabe nodded. 'Yeah, I thought that's what we were doing.

We can't seem to avoid that, can we? Maybe it's only a matter of time, then.'

The front door opened. 'Good, you're both here.'

Ash stepped away from Gabe, genuinely relieved to see her brother even if she had to turn her face away from him while she took a moment to calm the hell down.

'You're late.'

'Last meeting ran over.' He examined her face for a long moment when she looked at him. 'Something wrong?'

'No. Let's see these plans, then.'

'We need somewhere to lay them out—anything left we can make a table with, Gabe?'

Ash hung back as they built a makeshift table with boxes and part of a door, noting from her peripheral vision the very second Gabe came back to stand beside her while Alex rolled out the plans. Willing her heartbeat to return to the slow and steady rhythm she was really starting to miss, she looked sideways at him and found him doing the same to her, so she called him a name under her breath and prayed he'd heard it.

Running away again was getting pretty damn tempting.

When his table wobbled, Alex dragged another box over, and with the noise to mask his words Gabe leaned towards her, his gaze fixed forwards. 'Guess that just means we'll need to keep an eye on where the arguing leads us—unless you want to volunteer to get the next kiss out of the way sooner rather than later…'

He then calmly looked her straight in the eye and stepped forwards to help Alex.

So she stepped over to the table and concentrated on her brother's plans rather than contemplating murder in front of an eyewitness, 'We're still keeping as much of the old brickwork exposed as possible?'

'Yes, and where any new plasterwork is added the edges are

rough so it keeps that half-finished look to contrast with the new steel beams and the lighting.' Alex pointed a long finger at the paper. 'Mezzanine-level staircase is here. And access to the workshops upstairs is through a separate staircase accessible from below the mezzanine here and another door outside that your studio tenants can use here.'

'How long will the work take?'

'That's Gabe's territory.'

Alex nodded in his direction, so Ash was forced to look at him again—a part of her willing him to be the way he was with her in front of her brother so Alex could see he wasn't such a 'good guy' after all.

'Well?'

'Six weeks. Less if you're gonna be here every day. That's incentive enough on its own to get done faster.'

Alex grimaced. 'I took out the dividing wall you wanted here, Ash—so the Art Therapy room has more light.'

She smiled at him, grateful for the distraction. 'Good, it needs to be as bright and airy in there as possible. Where the wall was just made the room too small, you know?'

'Art Therapy?' Gabe directed the question at Alex.

But Alex merely shrugged and nodded at Ash, 'Ask Ash— it's her project. I just put the plans on paper and then you get to build it for her. Kinda makes us her dream team, if you think about it.'

She kept her eyes focussed on the plans, because if Gabe made fun of the Art Therapy then she'd never be able to forgive him. But neither could she look him in the eye if she had to explain it properly, because a part of her really didn't want him to know how much it meant to her. If they were still playing the 'hit where it hurts most' game, then it was major ammunition, being as close to her heart as it was.

Forcing her spine a little straighter, she kept her voice purposefully matter-of-fact. 'It's a way of getting kids and adults who've been traumatized through abuse, neglect, emotional problems or who have low self-esteem to express their feelings through art. I did volunteer work with a group in Paris attached to the college and they had great success with it there.'

'What was it—community service?'

She glanced up at Alex in time to see his jaw clench, sending a small smile of reassurance his way when he looked at her. 'Nope.'

'Don't the people who run those courses have to have some kind of specialist training?'

'I didn't run them, I helped out. And, yes, all the volunteers attended courses.' She silently cleared her throat. 'Personal experience counted too for some of the volunteers. I'm hoping it'll be the same here.'

When Gabe didn't make another comment she smiled at Alex again. 'These are great, Alex—really. Thanks.'

He bowed his head. 'You're very welcome. Your bill is in the post.'

'You have a payment plan?'

He smiled. 'I'll see what we can do.'

Gabe leaned in. 'My company prefers a cash advance.'

'You have a company all of your wee own-some?' Ash blinked up at him, refusing point-blank to budge an inch just because he'd moved in closer again.

'Yes.'

'With more than just the four employees you'll have working here?'

'Yes.'

Alex interrupted from the other side of the table. 'You two really should meet each other some time.'

Still looking up at Gabe, Ash crossed her arms. 'I suggested that but Gabe doesn't want to play.'

'Well, if you both tried swapping a little information it might help.' Alex waited for them both to glare at him, before he talked to them in a suitably appropriate tone for warring seven-year-olds, 'Gabe—you could tell Ash a little about your company. And, Ash—you could tell Gabe why the therapy group means so much to you that you're giving up the potential rental on half a floor—'

'Whose side are you on?'

'I'm not taking a side. You're my sister, he's one of my oldest friends and we work together—so that makes me Switzerland in this; I'm neutral.'

'So why does it mean so much, then?'

She ignored Gabe's question and continued staring at her brother. *How could he?*

At least he had the grace to look apologetic before he began to roll up the plans and tap them down into a leather cylinder. 'Maybe you should call a truce for the six weeks it'll take to get this place done.'

'Maybe you should try minding your own business.'

'Well, you see, I would, but I have to work with you two on this project. And I'm not acting as a go-between—I have enough problems of my own.'

He did? Mr Perfect? Mr Never-had-a-problem-his-whole-life? Alex had worn the Fitzgerald crown with ease at the same time his sister was out using it as collateral to get into the best clubs and parties.

She frowned at him. 'What kind of problems?'

'Woman problems I'll bet.'

She glared venomously at Gabe. 'Because we're the root of all evil, aren't we?'

'Would you listen to yourselves? It's pathetic.' The frustration in Alex's tone drew their attention back to him in time for him to point a finger at Gabe. 'He's built a successful construc-

tion company from the ground up while you've been away.'
Then at Ash. 'And she's been working with kids who have self-esteem issues because—'

'*Alex!*'

He shook his head. 'Fine. But you need to try talking to each other. It's when people don't talk that things get messed up.'

Ash felt her heart cramping up her chest at the sight of her brother hurting. Because he was, wasn't he? And even though he'd almost handed Gabe her deepest darkest secrets on a plate, she still couldn't stop herself from making an attempt to help when he looked so tortured, especially when it was so out of character. Tortured was *her* turf.

'Maybe you should try some of your own advice, big brother—ever think about that one?'

'She's as nuts about you as you are about her, you know.' Gabe joined Ash's 'team' for the first time in over a decade.

And Ash couldn't help but smile softly at him for it. 'It was pretty obvious at the party.'

Gabe smiled back at her. 'Bit nauseating, though.'

'Well, yes, from the outside it can be.'

'All right, you can stop now. I think I preferred it when you didn't agree.' Alex smiled too. 'Reminds me of the old days when you ganged up on me all the time.'

'Oh, yeah.' Ash laughed. 'Poor you. If you hadn't bullied me I wouldn't have needed protection in the first place. You brought it all on yourself.'

'You were the only girl. The boys were supposed to team up to pick on *you*—it's a right of passage thing.' He waved a hand at Gabe. 'Until you went all caped-crusader-defending-the-weaker-sex on me.'

'She was smaller than us. I just evened up the odds, was all.' He laughed the same kind of honest to goodness laugh he had when she'd found him in the hall with Moggie. 'And I did help you that time you hid all her clothes when we went midnight swimming.'

Ash dug him sharply in the ribs with her elbow. 'You told me you had nothing to do with that. And I had the cold for a week afterwards!'

'And didn't he bring you nice honey and lemon every night on demand to make up for it? The big *girl*…'

They laughed at the same time. And Ash felt as if she was home for the first time since she'd driven her car off the ferry. This was the kind of thing she'd missed the most—the three of them laughing together over shared history. But it had been Ash who had changed things; she knew that, just as she knew a part of her still ached for the loss of that closeness.

Alex took a deep breath, letting it out slowly before tucking his plans under one arm. 'Good times. We could do with remembering them more often now you're home, kiddo.'

She chanced a sideways glance at Gabe and found him looking down at her with a thoughtful expression on his face. And it was suddenly ridiculously sad to her that it took a third party to make them stand in the same room together without arguing.

'I gotta go—I'll see you guys later.'

Ash looked meaningfully at him. 'Talk to her.'

'Try not to kill each other while I'm not here.'

When Alex was gone, all of them having walked to the door *en masse*, together. And when Alex was gone, Ash took a breath before she made what she promised herself was a last attempt.

'So, a six-week truce, then.'

'Won't change the past.'

'Well, if you don't think you're up to it…'

'And you are?'

She shrugged. 'Only one way to find out.'

After another long moment of tense silence Gabe stepped

forwards, yanking open the door and holding it wide as he looked back at her with sunlight glinting off his tousled hair and an unreadable expression on his face. Then he surprised her by holding out a large hand. 'Gabe Burke.'

Ash stepped forward without second-guessing the move, placing her hand in his, watching as long fingers closed around hers, enveloping her in the kind of warmth that sent waves of awareness up the skin of her arm before she looked up into the blue of his eyes, replying with a small smile and a sure voice.

'Ashling Fitzgerald. People call me Ash when they're not calling me a pain in the ass.'

He smiled when she tossed his own words from the party at him. 'And are you?'

The answer to that would be some kind of test in his mind, wouldn't it? Well, one of the first things he'd have to learn was that she was well aware of her own failings—she didn't actually need someone to keep pointing them out to her.

So she nodded firmly, her hand still held in his. 'I can be, yes. But I like to hope it's not all of the time. *You?*'

'A pain in the ass?'

She nodded again, her smile growing. 'Yup.'

His gaze slid upwards, his full mouth pursing into a thin line as he considered his answer. 'Only when I feel it's called for.'

When he looked back into her eyes she held the steady gaze with one of her own. There was no question the next six weeks were still going to be a battle of wills, but suddenly it didn't seem all that torturous a prospect to her any more.

'Well…' she patted his upper arm with her free hand before reclaiming the one he held, tilting her head as she smiled a bright smile up at him, scrunching her nose a little while she nodded '…we can work on that.'

CHAPTER FOUR

GABE was discovering he might have underestimated just how much trouble Ash could be when she set her mind to it. Or maybe she just didn't realize her natural ability to *make* trouble for herself?

Somehow he doubted the latter.

Between the flirting and the innuendos and the never-ending selection of tight, figure hugging jeans and tops she appeared in every day he was doing pretty well not to throw her over a shoulder and lock her somewhere where she could stop distracting the hell out of his crew *and him*. Because at the present rate Alex's six week genius plan was going to stretch into three or four months easy, wasn't it?

And Gabe didn't fancy spending that long watching her at play. No matter how amusing he secretly found it from time to time when his guard slipped.

He watched as she laid the cards down on the table, a broad, deeply dimpled grin of triumph on her face as she gleefully announced, 'Read 'em and weep, boys—*royal flush*,' before she lifted both arms in the air and did a wiggling victory dance on her chair, her lithe body moving in a way that would have brought any guy's gaze to her full breasts in the figure-hugging green number she had on. At least that was what Gabe told himself when *he* looked.

Telling himself she should be used to men looking at her, he let himself look at her a little more. But when he started picturing her with less clothing on he knew it was time to stop…

Oh, she was trouble all right.

Frowning, he then checked the others to make sure their eyes weren't where his had been. Up until a couple of days ago they'd all have been looking an eyeful's worth. But this time there were merely several groans from around the makeshift table, so he shook his head as he gathered the cards back together.

'I should just pay their wages directly to you and save them the gloating.'

The lunch-break poker ritual had been gladly received by the crew, at the start. After all, a beautiful woman flirting her way into their good books brightened up the working day for them no end. They were never going to refuse anything she asked them to do with a bat of her long lashes and a sashay of her hips as she walked towards them—especially when she'd started providing mugs of tea, endless cakes and her sparkling wit to keep them company before she started fleecing them all.

But Gabe still wasn't entirely happy with the way they all flirted back with her while being fleeced. There was apparently a limit to how far his good humour stretched. And the fact he now knew there was bugged him.

'You're one of them card sharks, aren't you?' Sean, his foreman, grinned at her. 'It's as well you didn't agree to strip poker when we asked or we'd all be pretty cold by now.'

Gabe noticed the way Sean leaned a little closer to her. It was habit, that was all it was; even after so long he still had some kind of inbuilt radar when it came to guys hitting on Ash. And the urge to go yank her away and send her home was therefore a sort of Pavlov's dog type of conditioning.

'I warned you. But you lot wouldn't listen.' And the warning had been handed out with the kind of glare that said if they ever mentioned strip poker again they'd be working on projects outdoors in the dead of winter for the rest of their working days.

The hell he was sitting in a damn crowd if there was the slightest chance of her slowly peeling off one layer after another, revealing inch after inch of smooth skin and those long legs of hers and her full breasts and—

Now if it was one-on-one...well...he might even have been tempted to cheat for that kind of visual reward. But if looking at her with her clothes on had the effect on him it apparently did, then a naked Ash could well push him over the edge.

Thankfully the lads had dropped it.

And Ash had smiled knowingly.

Well she could think it meant she'd won something from him all she wanted, but she'd be wrong about that. Though, in fairness, her being around every day was helping to remind him of how much fun she could be when she set her mind to it. It was just a pity he knew the darker side of her personality, wasn't it?

She held a hand up to her ear, the gold flecks in her hazel eyes dancing with amusement. 'Oh, my, is that a hint of sore loser I can hear?'

He merely tapped the cards on the plasterboard and winked at her for the sheer hell of it. 'You know what they say about people who're unlucky with cards...'

She laughed huskily, looking him straight in the eye. 'I haven't seen any actual *evidence* of that.'

Gabe shot her a look filled with meaning—because she really didn't want to play that game with him, did she? But she simply lifted her chin in reply the way she always did when he challenged her.

'You wanna keep robbing my boys or would you like a place to hang nice pretty pictures before the next turn of century?'

The four other men took the hint and stood up.

Once they were out of earshot Ash flung an upwards glance at him while clearing up the leftovers and wrappers. 'They never say a bad word about you, you know. Pretty amazing, don't you think—considering they've *met* you.'

'Venturing out of truce territory there…'

'I've decided it maybe has something to do with the fact you get in there and do the work with them, which is a rare thing…' She nodded a sage-like nod.

So Gabe waited. Because there was more, wasn't there? There always was.

She stopped at his side, tilting her head back to study his mouth with the come-to-bed eyes he'd been finding so damned distracting of late, her voice low. 'You know, for someone who owns a company as large as Burke Developments and made it onto the Top Ten Most Eligible Bachelors in Ireland list last year…at number three no less.'

He took a deep breath filled with her scent, lowering his head and pausing for a heartbeat before dropping his voice. 'Number six on that list been singing my praises, has he?'

Ash looked into his eyes. 'Nope, haven't spoken to Alex the last few days—I "Googled" you.'

Gabe couldn't stop a burst of laughter breaking free from his chest. 'You "Googled" me?' He slapped a palm to his chest. 'I think I'm flattered.'

'Don't be—it's not like I have a poster of you on my bedroom wall or anything—though those pictures of you *were* flattering. Did they have to airbrush much?'

'Funny.' And, actually, the thought of Ash spending time researching his life *was* amusing to him. How the high and mighty had fallen. 'If you need to do a closer inspection to find out then just be nice to me and I'll see if I can pencil you in.'

'I'll just take your word for it.'

Gabe turned ninety degrees to tower over her. 'I wonder what we'd find if we "Googled" *your* name?'

She grimaced, but it was the way the light in her eyes died that made Gabe pause for thought. This truce thing wasn't a walk in the park, attempting to forget all his preconceptions so they didn't argue and risk the repercussions. And he knew he still regularly bent the rules and made digs. But it wasn't as if he could just erase the past and make like they really had just met. If he did he'd have to admit he'd just wounded her with the flippant question. And if her expression hadn't told him that then the flat tone in her voice when she answered him would have.

'I think we both know exactly what we'd find. And I'm fairly sure discussing it'll take us out of truce territory *at speed*.'

When she tried to move away Gabe reached out and took her hand without thinking, squeezing her fingers so that she looked up at him with her finely arched brows raised in question. He frowned again as he forced himself to continue playing to the rules.

'If we're playing "let's pretend" for six weeks and we'd just met I wouldn't know what I'd find, would I?' He kept his voice low. 'So you can tell me when I ask or I can "Google" you, like you felt you had to with me.'

He saw her throat convulse, looked back up and saw her damp her lips the way she always did when she was stalling for time or trying to test his patience. But when he looked back into her eyes he saw a flash of something he didn't recognize. Confusion? Wariness? No, he knew what those looked like. This was something new.

'So what would I find?'

She cleared her throat as if the words were hard to force out, avoiding his gaze as she answered in a husky tone that went straight to his gut.

'You'd find a girl on a path to self-destruction.' She smiled wryly into the middle distance. 'She almost made it too.'

His fingers tightened again.

But she'd already bounced back, freeing her hand from his as she leaned her head back.

'And one of the *joys* of the internet—' she rolled her eyes and grinned '—is that when I'm ninety all those gorgeous pictures will still be there for the world to see. And I'll never stand a bat's chance in hell of controlling my children or their children when they can throw them in my face and say, "But look what you did!"'

Gabe continued watching as she crinkled up her nose and made an exaggerated shiver of false glee, the bright smile still in place.

'Oh, yes, indeed; happy days yet to come.'

'And what'll you say to them?' He had no idea why the thought of her with kids of her own one day had never occurred to him. Or why the thought of her with them now made him look at her differently. 'Have you thought about that?'

He suspected she had, probably with a great deal of soul-searching judging by the act she'd just performed to hide how the thought of her sordid history being there for anyone to view for decades to come killed her. Dared he think it? Could the emotion he hadn't been able to recognize in her eyes have been remorse? Maybe even a sense of shame.

If either one then he really didn't know the woman in front of him that well, did he? Because the Ash he'd known didn't give a damn about anyone or anything but herself. And anyone foolish enough not to see that before they got sucked in by her blatant sexuality, constant spark of mischief and hedonistic love of all things good would get tossed over her shoulder the second the wind changed. Gabe knew because he'd watched her do it time and time again without *any* shame *or* remorse.

The phrase 'wild child' could have been coined specifically for her; she'd worn it that well.

'Maybe I'll just send them round to their uncle Gabe's house and they can learn everything about life from he-who-knows-all.'

It might have been said with a teasing light in her eyes, but Gabe chose to rise to the bait yet again. 'So they can see the difference between the girl who had everything and the guy who had to work his way up from the lower classes?'

The smile faded. 'You still have a really noticeable chip on your shoulder—you know that, don't you?'

'I wonder how it might have got there?'

To her credit she didn't let his knee-jerk response lead her into the kind of comeback that would break the truce before he did. Instead she broke eye contact, turning her profile to him.

'It was there before I used it against you, Gabe—I think we both know that's true. And we might both know exactly why I used it if we thought about it. But that's an argument all over again, isn't it?'

'It's maybe as well we have a truce in place, then.'

Ash flashed him another, smaller smile. 'Especially when we already hate each other as much as we do.'

'Exactly.'

The usual heavy rock music was blaring from the new mezzanine level when the rest of Gabe's crew popped their heads round her door to say goodnight—joking about how they'd get their money back in the next day's game.

And then, after much inner debate as to whether or not it was a good idea, Ash caved in, closed her laptop down and went looking to see what Gabe was doing. It was her project after all—she had a right to see how it was coming along. It had nothing to do with the fact that for ten or fifteen minutes after the crew left, when they'd talk about the safe subject of the gallery, they actually managed a conversation without any attempts at pushing the truce.

The music was even louder upstairs, which meant she was able to stand on the top stair with her hand still on the rail watching him without him knowing she was there.

She'd been doing a lot of that lately…

Every guy on the face of the planet who looked like he did should wear work clothes, she'd decided after his first day on the job. Especially if they looked as good in them as Gabe did—not that he wasn't equally good-looking in a tux, mind you, but there was just something very *male* about a man dressed down and not caring if he was dirty. It was a primal thing, she supposed; a *sexual* thing. Most likely because it involved the word 'dirty'.

She watched the muscles in his forearm flex as he forced the lid off a tin of paint, had to squint to force herself not to ogle him when he bent over to grab a paintbrush. And when he lifted the end of his T-shirt to rub dust off his face she frowned as she got a tempting glimpse of the kind of abs that probably garnered the 'six-pack' label.

People who didn't like other people really shouldn't find them so tempting, should they?

'Don't you have a home to go to?'

He glanced over his shoulder when she turned the music down, 'I could ask you the same thing.'

'I'm on my way out. Moggie has been locked up all afternoon so I fully expect several soft furnishings to have died a horrible death.'

'I still don't think you can call a dog Moggie. He has to have enough of a complex with his breed name.'

'Labradoodles are very popular, I'll have you know.' She stepped closer, forcing her gaze off his tousled hair and onto the wall he was working at while she stepped closer. 'Are those the colors for the plastered parts of the walls?'

He focused on the three wide test stripes as she reached his side. 'They can dry overnight and you can pick one tomorrow before I order a job lot.'

'Isn't it all going to be white?' She crossed her arms while they both studied the stripes, determined not to glance over at him. She'd been watching him entirely too much of late and it was already bugging her beyond belief, as was her constant awareness of where he was the second he got within distance of her, catching a hint of his scent. 'None of those are white.'

'Yeah, they are.'

'No, they're not.'

'Yeah, they are.' He leaned his upper body her way, dropping his voice as if it were some kind of state secret. 'It says so on the tins.'

Ash made the mistake of looking at him, only to find his eyes sparkling dangerously, and her pulse immediately skipped a beat in response—dammit. And there was no reason to get all hot and bothered when what he was doing for the gazillionth time was goading her into a response. It was his favorite pastime, after all. Whether it was dropping something into a conversation that tested the truce, or smiling at her when she least expected him to so she was left wondering what he found so flipping amusing, or just plain challenging her with that devilish sparkle in his eyes the way he was right that second.

It was unnerving, it kept her on edge all the damn time, and she hated him for it. Because he *knew* what he was doing; almost as if he wanted her to hate him as much as he despised her, which he still did, no matter how many times he smiled at her.

Unfolding her arms, she bent over to read the side of the tin. 'Apple white.' She smirked at him, set it down and got another.

'Barley white.' Another tin. 'O-h-h-h, and what do we have here? Why, it's *champagne white*. None of those are white, Gabriel.'

He turned ninety degrees. 'Still says white.'

'Still *not* white.' She smiled sweetly. 'And you know that or you wouldn't be making stripes of each one for me to choose from, would you?'

'*Ah*, but, you see—' he stepped closer, his deep voice giving the innocent words undertones all over again '—one is *gloss*, one is *matt*, and the other is *soft sheen*. Still white—different finishes.'

She studied his face, her gaze dropping from his eyes to the wide sweep of his full mouth, along the thick column of his neck to his broad chest, a mischievous imp of old gleefully presenting her with a way to prove her point.

'Your T-shirt is white, isn't it?'

'Was before I started work today.'

'Okay, then.' She lifted the paintbrush out of the tin she was holding, calmly splattered paint across his chest and smiled again. 'Now you can see that champagne white *isn't* white. There's a hint of *gold* in there…'

His thick lashes rose slowly, his voice holding an edge of warning that made her pulse skip again. 'Trust me when I tell you, you *really* didn't want to do that.'

Ash batted her eyelashes at him. 'Really? And why would that be?'

Gabe pursed his mouth and she could almost *feel* the very instant he made the decision to get his own back. So she dipped her paintbrush back into the tin, a bubble of laughter building in her chest. Her heart thudded a little louder, her breathing changed, and she recognized the sensations as the beginning of the all too familiar thrill of anticipation. That addictive rush of adrenaline in her veins she'd always sought out when she couldn't deal with something else. And it had always, *always* got her in trouble before.

It was his fault, she told herself. He would keep pushing her back into her old habits.

Her chin rose defiantly. 'I was just proving a point. Is it *my* fault you're colour-blind?'

'So tell me, just out of curiosity—what colour would you say that nice top of yours is?'

Ash backed away as he calmly bent over to lift a tin, fighting back the growing bubble of laughter as she went. 'This *beautiful* top is aubergine. Not just purple—but *aubergine*. 'Cos there are different shades of purple too, you know.'

'Not gonna be *aubergine* for long.'

'Careful now—there's still a truce in place here.'

'Well, if you stand still we'll be even for this one in about two seconds.'

The hell they would.

The first splatter missed, but not by much, and the second came so fast she barely had time to react. When it hit her squarely across her breasts she gasped, looking up at his smiling face as he smugly informed her, '*Now* we're even.'

The hell they were.

She lifted her brush, ignoring him when he said her name in a warning tone, and then battle commenced in earnest, Ash's heart leaping ridiculously when he laughed the kind of laugh she liked best—even while she was ducking and diving to avoid the onslaught and the floor got slippery beneath her feet.

The bubble of laughter in her chest grew too large to contain. But the second it broke free Gabe used his immense size to his advantage, crowding her back against the wall, holding up a heavily laden brush dripping paint in slow motion onto the floor beside them.

Dark brows disappeared beneath thick locks of equally dark hair. 'You done?'

'Are *you*?' Her heart thundered hard against her breastbone, the answering question a little on the breathless side.

'You first.'

'That's very chivalrous of you, but in this age of emancipation I'd have to say no, really...*you first*...'

Gabe pursed his lips, took a deep breath that brought the wide wall of his chest dangerously close to her breasts, then, exhaling as he stepped back, lowered his arm to lazily paint a wide stripe across the waist of her once-aubergine top.

Ash tried to squirm out of the way, but he seemed to know where she was moving before she moved—blocking every attempt and using his free arm to stop her from getting her own brush back into play. Until Ash went still and just let him paint her until his brush was almost dry.

'Okay. You win. But only because you played the stronger-species card.'

Gabe waited until her arms dropped to her sides before dipping his paintbrush back in his tin, his deep voice low and calm. 'You need to learn you can't win with me.'

And he didn't just mean in a paint fight, did he?

Ash's lashes lowered to watch as he moved his brush around the tin in slow circles, as if loading it up for another onslaught. And then she looked up, absent-mindedly studying a splash of white that was clinging to his hair while she spoke. 'And it's always going to be a battle with us, isn't it?'

He didn't look at her. 'Yup.'

She sighed in frustration, watching his thick lashes flicker up as he looked at her face for a split second—just long enough for her to see his eyes darken to a deeper blue—and then her breath caught as his gaze dropped again, his brush lifting to begin painting a pattern across her breasts.

His mouth curved into a slow, purely sexual smile. And Ash stayed frozen to the spot, her eyes closing as she tried to stifle the need to groan—until it suddenly hit her what he was doing.

'Are you writing your *name* on me?'

'Yup.'

His low chuckle of laughter forced her eyes open while he pushed the brush firmer against her breast as he formed the letter 'B'. And for the life of her Ash couldn't understand why she stood still and *let* him.

Especially when her disobedient body was reacting to the slow movement of the brush and the flicker of his thick lashes as he watched what he was doing. She even felt her breasts tingle when the brush lifted, her deep breath lifting them towards him as if silently inviting him to continue.

People who didn't like other people *did not* give them any kind of a come-on, *dammit*!

But it was too late to hide her reaction, because his lashes had already lifted, he was already searching her eyes and she knew the second he knew. Because a small frown formed, his eyelids grew heavy, and his mouth formed a mocking smile. *Bastard.*

'I hate you.'

The smile twitched, his voice a gravelly rumble from deep in his chest. 'I know.'

When she tried to push off the wall, he stepped in and held her in place by simply standing there, his gaze flickering over her face and taking in what she could feel was a flush on her cheeks and what she assumed would be a sparkling anger in her eyes.

And she hated him even more for the fact her laughter sounded nervous, 'O-h-h-h, I don't think you do.'

Brush in one hand, tin swinging from the other, he leaned his knuckles against the wall on either side of her head, his face lowering towards hers—his intense gaze focussed on her eyes. 'You hate the fact that I know you as well as I do.'

'I hate the fact you still *think* you do.'

His warm breath, scented with a hint of mint, washed over her cheeks, his voice dropping an octave. 'You hate that there's no way to avoid me.'

She tried to squirm free, more forcibly this time. But he pushed his hips in against the curve of her stomach—and Ash inhaled sharply at the jolt the contact sent through her nerve endings.

Gabe lowered his head further, moving to one side so that his words rumbled close to her ear. 'And that right this minute you're turned on when you don't want to be.'

'*Yes.*' The word was forced from between clenched teeth, and she didn't even have time to clarify that she meant the hating part rather than the turned-on part, because he'd already nudged her hair out of the way with his nose—his lips so close to her ear that she thought she could feel them moving.

The truth was, it was yes to both, wasn't it?

'So you'd hate it if I kissed you, wouldn't you?'

'Yes, I would.' Her bottom lip trembled on the lie, so she bit down on it, *hard*. Needing the physical pain as a reminder, because she wouldn't just hate him for kissing her—she'd hate herself for so badly wanting him to. If what his words and his proximity could do to her body were any indication, then she doubted she'd be able to stop herself from getting lost in it, from—Lord help her—wanting more.

And people who hated other people as much as she hated him would *never* sleep with them. Even if just thinking about it sent their body up in flames.

'It's just as well I'm not going to, then, isn't it?' He pushed against the wall, examining her face with hooded eyes before he took the tin from her hand and moved across the room. 'Go home, Ash.'

After a couple of shaky breaths, she forced her chin high and started towards the stairs, her hand on the rail when she stopped, turning her head just enough to see his broad back from her peripheral vision.

'If you wanted me to hate you as much as you hated me for what I did all those years ago, then you've just done a pretty good job, Gabe.' She swallowed hard so the emotion didn't show in her voice.

'*Now* we're even.'

CHAPTER FIVE

THE Temple Bar quarter was filling up fast with the usual crowd of Dubliners glad to be free from their desks for a few days when they walked into the pub on Friday night. Sean raised his voice to be heard.

'You and Ash have a bit of a row by any chance, boss?'

Gabe scowled hard when he looked to see who Sean had waved at. And it wasn't just the sight of Ash lifting her hand to wave back that made him scowl—it was the cursory glance to see who she was with.

Hadn't taken long for her to fall back in with her old social circle, had it?

'Don't call me boss when we're off the clock.' He turned his back on the motley crew from her school days, setting his foot on the brass runner along the bottom of the wooden bar before shooting a sideways glance at Sean. 'Been bending your ear, has she?'

'Nah.' Sean leant his elbows on the wood while Gabe signalled for the barman. 'But she's not been herself, has she? You'd know, knowing her as long as you have. And the lads have missed her the last coupla days—she brightens up the place.'

And the fact that the crew had all been treating her as if she'd suffered a bereavement before she disappeared hadn't gone unnoticed by Gabe. They'd taken to trying to make her laugh at every opportunity they got and that was almost as distracting as her being there in the first place had been, so he'd taken to cracking the whip more than he usually did, which led to the need to buy them all a drink to ease his conscience…

After all—they weren't the cause of his bad humour.

But he'd be damned if she was going to make him feel guilty for his actions. No matter how much she'd seemed to withdraw into herself since the night he'd so very nearly kissed her.

'Well, maybe she'd cheer up if we got the place finished ahead of schedule?'

Sean lifted a hand to salute him. *'Yessir!'*

Gabe laughed.

The rest of the crew arrived, and with pints equally distributed they settled into the usual back and forth about football and cars. But Gabe couldn't relax the way he normally did at the end of a working week, his eyes straying to the group of women less than twenty feet away from them.

One caught sight of him, her eyes widening in surprise. So Gabe smiled a slow smile and raised his glass in salute, chuckling as he turned back to the lads. Because he'd just bet there was about to be an interesting conversation at *that* table.

'Oh, my God—is that your gardener's son?'

Ash looked over at the bar, frowning at the sight of the group of women who'd gravitated towards Gabe and co. Not that standing there towering over every other man in the bar while wearing a black leather jacket and jersey combo with faded blue jeans—lending him quite the bad-boy look when accompanied by his unruly dark hair and sparkling baby blues—wasn't an open invitation to every woman with a pulse to run over and introduce herself at breakneck speed.

'It is, isn't it?'

It'd been the longest evening of her life already, and Meredith's question was the icing on the cake. Just went to prove the old adage of 'never look back', really, didn't it? But it would have been rude not to accept the invitation from her old school friends—though the term 'friends' could be used loosely, Ash felt.

'No, he's—' She frowned harder when she almost did what he was constantly accusing her of doing: relegating him to some kind of antiquated station in life rather than who he was.

'Gabriel Burke.' Catriona nudged Meredith with a smug smile, 'And as if you don't know rightly who he is. He has more money than your family does these days. Did you see him in that eligible bachelors thing last year? Be still my beating heart…'

Ash watched as Cat smiled in rapture, her eyes narrowing as she fanned her face with a waving hand. Cat by name…

Meredith didn't look amused; it was probably the dig about the money that'd done it. That was the thing about old titled families—they might have their titles and the big old rambling houses, but those self-same rambling houses had bled a lot of them dry over the centuries. Whereas Gabe was a self-made man, he was what her 'friends' considered 'new money'. It meant he was more likely to mix in their circles than before, but, even diluted down by each generation as it was, some of the old snobbery still existed.

And Ash hated it almost as much as she hated the way they were talking about Gabe. 'He's worked hard to build his company.'

'*Companies*, darling. His holding company owns properties all over Dublin now, didn't you know?' Cat practically purred the words at her. 'And he's quite the playboy these days. You should have held on tighter back in the days when he had his eye on you.'

'He *is* gorgeous.' Pam—or the Right Honourable Mr John Carmichael's Mrs Pamela Carmichael née Hayes—if Ash had it straight that was—leaned closer to her. 'And Meredith would have to agree, of course…'

What did *that* mean? Ash opened her mouth to ask only to have Meredith lift her nose in the air and announce, 'He can be as sexy as sin but it doesn't change his background, does it? It's a Lady Chatterley thing.'

The others laughed raucously, but Ash could feel acid building in her stomach. 'Did you even notice the change of century we had? It was a few years ago but the sight of all those horseless carriages everywhere must have been a hint for you?'

'Darling, we're only joking—'

'No, you're not.' She knew she was about to lose a few 'friends' whose families regularly socialized with her own, but quite frankly she didn't give a damn. 'You all think you're better than him. And you're not—none of us are. Gabe made his money through hard work; didn't have it handed down to him or feel the need to marry into it. So, actually, that makes him better than us.'

Cat's eyes narrowed again, her voice now coated in sugar. 'Correct me if I'm wrong, but weren't you the one who put him in his place in front of all of us when—?'

'I was a spoilt brat who'd just had her socks kissed off and didn't know what to do about it! And what I did and said was cruel and uncalled for.'

'Yes, well, I'd imagine you *would* regret it *now*—' Cat jerked her head in the direction of the bar '—when he's as sexy and successfully as that today. But you can't tell me that your family would approve of a Fitzgerald actually *marrying* someone—'

Ash laughed out loud. 'Oh, Cat—*darling*—since when was

I happy about being a Fitzgerald? I spent years making sure to bring the family name into disrepute; you know that.' She smiled a saccharine-sweet smile of her own. 'You were right there with me for a long time, if you recall. I even have you to thank for the introduction to Dev; now *there's* a guy to show us what having good breeding means, right?'

Pam's voice was brittle. 'We all make mistakes when we're too young to know better.'

'Yes.' Ash nodded, her lips a tight line as she swallowed down her anger. 'But as adults we should have the wit to learn from them. So you'll have to excuse me, 'cos I'd rather go stand over at the bar with Gabe and his crew than sit here and listen to you lot decide if indentured servants should be brought back.'

Devil and the deep blue sea maybe, but she *would* rather stand with the man who had a reason to dislike her than the three women who deep down thought she'd just done what had to be done to put him back in his 'place'. Maybe if she'd had the maturity back in the day she'd have laughed *at them* rather than *with them* at him.

Gabe was at the jukebox and had one hand flipping through the track listings, the other fishing in his pocket for change when she got to him. But even when she leaned her shoulder against the old-fashioned machine, he didn't so much as look at her, he just waited—and she hated him for being so unaffected by her presence.

'Hey.'

He continued flipping through the tracks. 'To what do I owe the honour?'

'Just pretend we get along until that lot leave, Gabe, and then I'll go. I *promise* not to cramp your style even the teensiest little bit, okay.'

'Why?'

A quick glance saw her scowl hard before she folded her arms beneath her breasts. 'Just because.'

He shook his head. 'You want to get into an argument about me and Meredith, then you can forget it. It's none of your business.'

'You and *Meredith*? The Meredith that's *married*?'

'She wasn't married then.' He shrugged, slotted coins into the machine and punched a couple of the buttons, the disc dropping down into place and an aggressive, heavy rock beat kicking in.

Forcing Ash to step closer and raise her voice to be heard. 'She wasn't married *when*?'

'Still none of your business.'

'Should I ask about the rest of them too?'

'Depends. Do you want to be told that's none of your business either?'

She stepped closer still, the tip of her breast brushing against his arm. And he frowned at the jukebox, because he didn't want to be aware of the fact her breast was touching him, or the fact that her standing on her toes to yell into his ear sent sweet vanilla undertones into the air around him.

'What'd you do, Gabe—track them all down after I left for a little *revenge sex*?'

He laughed at the idea and then rocked a little sideways when she punched him in the arm. In the split second it took to realize she was leaving he reached out, curling his arm around her narrow waist to haul her in against his side, his fingers splaying wide on the inward curve of her back.

'Oh, no you don't.' He turned his face so his mouth was close enough to her ear for her to hear him over the music. 'Not before you tell me exactly what the problem is. 'Cos to the un-trained eye you might look jealous…'

He felt her burst of laughter against his side, had to lift his head to hear her answer. 'I'm so-o-o pleased I felt the need to defend you five minutes ago!'

When he leaned back further to try and look into her eyes, she turned her face away, pulling back against his arm. But he simply held her tighter, leaning down to her ear again. 'And why would you do that?'

'Damned if I know!'

She'd turned her head to shout the words, but when he tried to see her face again, she turned away—again. And Gabe was rapidly losing patience. 'Look at me, Ash.'

She leaned back against his arm. He moved her round so that her body was held tight against his—her breasts crushed against his chest while he frowned at the crowd and backed them towards a darker corner. And when he was sure they didn't have too much of an audience, he lifted his free hand to her chin, fingers forcing her to face him so he could look into her eyes.

Reflected light made it look as if her eyes were shimmering, and he frowned all the harder. Because it had to be anger glittering there, not hurt—it was just that he couldn't see clearly enough, was all.

'Why exactly was it you felt you had to defend me?'

'Go to hell.'

'What happened over there?'

Her lower lip trembled. And he saw it clearly, even in the dim light, so he knew he wasn't seeing something that wasn't there. But it still didn't explain why she was so upset. He just didn't get it.

And then she astounded him further by asking, 'Did I turn you into some kind of *monster*? Or is this who you really are and I'm the only one lucky enough to get to see the real you?'

Right, he'd had enough. Releasing her, he grabbed her hand, tugging her behind him to the nearest exit door—the door he slammed open with his palm before dragging her out into the busy street, then around the corner into a deserted alley.

'Let me go, Gabe.'

'The hell I will.' He stopped dead in his tracks and hauled her round in front of him. 'You're gonna tell me what that meant.'

Ash tried to shake her hand free, lifting her other hand to angrily tug at the strands of hair caught in her lashes when he swung her round. 'Why? You wanted me to hate you, didn't you?'

'I didn't go tracking your friends down for *revenge sex*.' The fact he felt the need to tell her that much only made him angrier. 'If it's so important you know, then *yes*—I had a thing with Meredith. But she came looking for me long before I made the mistake of kissing *you* and when she came looking again after you left I followed it through. But it's got nothing to do with you and it's still none of your business.'

Ash's eyes widened. '*She* chased after *you*?'

Gabe laughed sarcastically. 'Oh, yeah—'cos why in hell would she do that, right? When I was so beneath her...' He stepped in and threw the words in her face. 'Maybe she wasn't as fussy about who she had fun with as you were. Maybe she got exactly what she wanted out of it. And maybe it was me that ended it, not her.'

She leaned towards him, throwing back angry words of her own. 'Did it occur to you for a single second that I might be more concerned about her doing something to hurt *you* rather than the other way round?'

'And when did you ever give a damn about the idea of me getting hurt?'

The glitter in her eyes was easier to see under the streetlights, the crack in her voice easier to hear in the quiet alley. 'How about every single day of my childhood from the moment I was able to say your name?'

It was a sucker punch. And it caught him right in the gut, rocking him back a little on his heels. But his recovery rate was good, even if the anger had been kicked out of him and replaced with the control he'd learned long ago to exert—the very control it'd taken to keep him from having some of that angry sex he'd briefly considered having with her.

'Well, you grew out of it, didn't you?'

Her breath caught. She stepped back from him as if he'd just sucker-punched her the same way she had him. And when she spoke she had the exact same deathly calm edge to her voice.

'That's just the thing.' She shook her head, kept backing away. 'If I had then I wouldn't have spent all these years regretting the day I hurt you. And if you knew me as well as you think you do—you'd know that.'

He found his feet carrying him forwards. 'You don't care about me, you hate me.'

'Because you do everything you can to *make* me hate you— because *you* hate *me*.'

'And yet we still can't seem to stay the hell away from each other, can we? We keep ending up *arguing*.'

'Changing nothing…'

''Cos you can't undo the damage once it's done…'

She stopped backing away, her chin lifting, her gaze locking with his. 'Not when there's no getting past it.'

When he was right in front of her, towering over her, he lifted his hands to her face to tilt her head further back. And when her long lashes rose, she swallowed hard and then—and only then—did he begin to question what he'd thought he'd known.

Circles. They were going round in circles with every argument and each circle—

He mumbled the words against her lips. 'Brings us back to where this started…'

CHAPTER SIX

ASH couldn't make out the words, but there wasn't time to try and figure them out, because the second Gabe's mouth met hers she *couldn't* think. He was doing it again, wasn't he?

It was like standing in a storm.

He wasn't tentative with her, wasn't gentle, didn't take time to discover the shape of her mouth; as if he'd kissed her a thousand times instead of just the once.

But with the whirlwind of emotions she felt twisting round and round inside her chest she didn't want gentle. She leaned into the kiss—sought his mouth as if she were seeking oxygen having been underwater for too long—hands reaching to grab handfuls of the dark leather against his back.

And when she met each demand his firm lips made with demands of her own, Gabe made a low, growling sound in the base of his throat and pushed the long fingers of one hand back from her face and into her hair, angling her head to deepen the kiss.

People who hated other people shouldn't immediately be as ragingly turned on by kissing them as she was, should they? *Should they?* How did that make any sense?

And why in hell wasn't she fighting him off, slapping him, asking, 'How could you?' As she'd ended up doing last time.

But it wasn't like last time, was it? This time she understood what the whisper was across her nerve endings, what the sensation of having the blood in her veins turn to fire meant, what her body sought where it had begun to bunch up and tighten in anticipation.

Because as a fully grown woman she knew what wanting a man felt like. She just hadn't ever experienced it on such an overwhelming scale, barring that one other time...

His fingers flexed against the back of her head, his mouth lifted from hers—and for a second she even swayed forwards, her mouth following his.

When she managed to open her eyes she found him staring down at her, his face still a matter of inches away. And she knew in a second he would tell her it was a mistake, or that he'd won this battle by proving how easily he could control her with just one kiss. He'd say something to make her hate him all over again. And she didn't want him to...

'Don't...'

The spark of misunderstanding in his eyes was swift, an answering frown following fast. 'Don't *what*? Don't—'

Not this time.

She yanked an arm round, reached up, fingers curling around the wide column of his neck to draw him close while she forced out the word again. '*Don't.*'

When she ran the tip of her tongue over his bottom lip, he made another low growling noise in his chest. But when his fingers flexed tighter against her head and he deepened the kiss she knew it wasn't a growl of protest. Whatever else was wrong between them, this one thing was right—oh-so-right. He was a lifeline in the storm, his large body an anchor she needed desperately to hold onto.

So she did, sinking into him, pressing her breasts tight against the wall of his chest while she stepped in the one last step to close what distance there was left between them. And when his tongue met hers, pushed in and tangled, she almost moaned aloud—immediately lifting her other hand from his back to push her fingers into his unruly hair, urging him closer.

Gabe's large hands dropped from her face and untangled from her hair, moving lower, skimming the sides of her body, moulding inwards with the curve of her waist and then out to the flare of her hips. His fingers splayed wide, and then flexing hard before hauling her even tighter against him; her pelvis now snug against his thighs, his hardening length cradled against her stomach.

And Ash *did* moan then, because it was too much and not enough at the same time. She wanted—no, she *needed*—she just—dammit it wasn't enough! She wanted to throw caution to the four winds and sample the heat that had been there between them for weeks now; she wanted to go somewhere where she could strip layers of clothes off him and touch him properly, she wanted him to do the same to her until—

She just *wanted*.

As if he could hear her, his hands moved round, sliding under the light material of her blouse, long fingers splaying again—this time against her hot skin. He exerted pressure against the small of her back, pushing her harder against his erection so that she moaned again—begging for more without using any words. Words were their downfall, after all; words had got in the way of everything else, from that one horrendous night onwards.

Rejecting him last time had been the beginning of a downward spiral it had taken years for her to climb her way back out of. When maybe if she'd just hung onto him...

She felt the tension start at the back of his neck, felt his chest heave as he drew in a deep breath, but even though she tried to get closer still to hang onto the moment, it was too late. He was already moving his hands back to her hips—setting her back from him before he tore his mouth from hers and set her back further still.

When she looked up at him, her hands falling from his neck and his hair to her sides, she saw a flash of anger in his eyes, saw the way his darkened gaze focussed on her tingling lips. And she damped them in response, running the tip of her tongue over the swollen flesh as if trying to keep the taste of him in her mouth.

Gabe made another lower growl in reply, lifting a hand to run it through his hair and down over his face before he examined the wall behind her, almost as if he'd find answers there to whatever questions he was silently asking.

Then, 'What is it you think you want from me?'

She swallowed. 'I don't know.'

'I think you do.'

Fixing his gaze on hers, he stepped forward while Ash consciously stood her ground, her chin tilting up as he narrowed his eyes, smiled cruelly and continued pushing. 'I think you want forgiveness for the past. I think that's why you came home to begin with. And I think you want to finish what we started on that swing that night.'

'Are you gonna tell me right this second that idea doesn't hold a certain appeal to you too?' She nodded her head in the direction of the ridge below his waist. 'I'm not the only one turned on, am I?'

Blunt honesty only made him scowl darkly. 'You think you can make up with me like this? Try and put things back the way they were before. Is that what this is?'

'So you can have more revenge sex?' She asked the question with a small burst of laughter so he could see she didn't really believe it was something he'd already done. And she didn't, not really. Because she might not be all that familiar with the new

Gabe, but the Gabe she'd once known would never even have contemplated it, would he? He'd been too honourable.

But then what did *she* know? She felt as if she didn't know *anything* any more. Not after that kiss. Not when she was standing looking at him and wanting that kiss all over again and with a need as vitally important as the one for oxygen.

'You'd offer yourself up for that, would you? You'd sink that low?' His voice rose. 'You think I want some kind of sacrificial offering in my bed?'

He was doing it again, wasn't he?

'You'd just love me to say yes to that, wouldn't you? 'Cos if I said yes—if I said it'd be worth it—maybe you'd think we really were even that way. You could just hate me some more, couldn't you? 'Cos I'd be the low-life without morals or feelings you already think I am.'

She couldn't possibly want someone who thought that way about her, could she? How self-destructive would that still make her, even after so many years?

He swore viciously, pacing up and down and searching the sky before he eventually stopped, looked her in the eye and said, 'I don't think you don't have morals.'

The words were said on so low a grumbling tone she almost missed them, were accompanied by a following dark scowl and his need to break eye contact for a brief moment so she knew he wasn't happy having said them aloud. But she *had* heard them, and the fact he was annoyed at having said them meant they were true.

And Ash felt a wave of longing sweep over her, so strong it made her weak at the knees.

'But you do think I'm worthless, don't you?' She tried to hide how much that hurt behind another burst of laughter, turning her face away to blink back threatening tears. 'The irony is, for a long time I'd have agreed with you on that one. It took me years to believe anything different.'

When she glanced his way he was frowning down at her again, eyes still searching hers.

In for a penny as the saying went. 'So no matter how low your opinion of me is, *trust me* when I tell you it can't be any lower than mine was.' She pointed her arm in the direction of the wall. 'And that lot in there just reminded me of one of the things I hated most about myself when they talked about you the way they did.'

'So you thought you'd right some of the past wrongs by defending me now when you didn't then?'

She laughed again, the sound harsher this time as she let her arm drop back to her side. 'No doubt that's a case of too little too late in your book. It's that whole "you saint, me sinner" thing again, isn't it? Well, you know what?'

She pursed her still sensitive lips together, dug down deep inside for the strength to stop herself shedding a single tear in front of him or reaching out for him again, and held her head even higher as she informed him, 'You've spent years working your ass off to prove to the world what you're capable of being—no matter what your start in life was. What we're born to doesn't make us who we are. Maybe I'd just like the chance to prove the same thing.'

'I'm not stopping you.'

'Yes, you are.' She shook her head. 'How can you not see that? You're like some kind of constant reminder of what I used to be.'

His upper body leaned in a little closer so it would have taken very little to reach for him if she let herself. 'Maybe you need that reminder. Maybe that's why you didn't push me away when I kissed you this time.' The words washed over her with an almost dangerous seductiveness. 'Maybe you want to put the clock back and follow through on what we had that one time to see if it makes everything better in the here and now.'

Was that the reason she'd responded to him the way she just had? Hadn't she thought something similar when she was standing in the storm? If there hadn't been that physical response, that longing inside, that *need*—would kissing him have felt as good as it had? Would she have felt as if she should cling onto it this time and not let go?

Ash decided she didn't want to keep analyzing things that deeply, not when it was turning her inside out the way it was. 'Maybe when kissing someone feels that good, that's all there is to it. You tried to tell me that once and you managed to forget how much you hate me for a few minutes just now, didn't you? And maybe that's what we need to do, Gabe—focus all that emotion somewhere else when it gets too strong and—'

'Kiss it better?' He looked both stunned and amused by the idea at the same time, damn him. The quirk of his dark brows challenging her to realize just what it was she was suggesting.

So she did what she always did and rose to the bait. *'Maybe. Maybe the best way not to feel so much anger all the time is to try to feel something else in its place.'*

'Like pleasure?' His voice dropped an octave, the sparkle that had been humour in his eyes changing to something altogether different.

And her answer was more than a little breathless in response. 'Maybe.'

'So every time we get into an argument we stop ourselves from saying what we really wanna say by kissing? Or touching? Or *what*?' His voice rose with each suggestion. 'How far do we go, Ash? Do we have some good old-fashioned angry sex against the nearest available wall? You tell me—what exactly is it you *want*?'

His harsh words fuelled her frustration beyond belief so she ended up yelling her answer back at him. *'I don't know!'*

He yelled too. 'And that's been half your problem your whole damn life, hasn't it?'

She closed her eyes, feeling the agony of an old wound forcibly reopened so soul-deep it took a minute of deep breathing before she felt she could speak again. When she looked at Gabe he was clenching his jaw, anger radiating from him in waves while she hid behind a shield of flat-toned words.

'Sex against the nearest wall? Is that what it's gonna take to satisfy you?'

She saw his hands bunch into fists at his sides, but when he didn't say anything she looked back into his eyes and challenged him with what she hoped to the bottom of her heart was the truth.

'But you can't take revenge even if a part of you really wants to because you remember when we were close, don't you? You remember it just as well as I do.'

And maybe the very reason she'd even suggested they replace the anger with something else was because she knew he wouldn't take her up on it? And by not taking her up on it he'd be proving that he *did* still care enough to not let her sell herself short that way?

Was she testing him now?

But she knew a big part of the reason behind it was she couldn't cope with the sexual attraction she had for him. No matter how she tried, it just wouldn't go away. It had spilled over into the kiss she could still feel on her lips and even after their angry words she could still feel the tug towards him. She still knew that if he reached for her again she wouldn't stop him. He was making her insane and she hated him for it!

Gabe towered over her again, so many things flickering across his sparkling blue eyes and so fast that she didn't have time to try and read them before they were replaced by something else. Was he fighting some kind of battle with himself now? Trying to decide whether or not to throw more angry words at her or to give into what they'd given into only minutes before?

Ash ached not knowing. She just *ached*.

And it must have shown in her eyes, because he shook his head, turned round—and walked away from her.

So she watched him leave, watched his long stride and the set of his broad shoulders, watched him kick something from under his feet before he turned out of the alleyway. And she smiled tremulously, looked heavenwards and let out a short burst of laughter that sounded distinctly like a sob. Because even though she was left aching all the way down to her bones, he hadn't let her sell herself into a sordid affair either, had he? And that had to mean something, didn't it?

Gabe walked around for hours or it might have been minutes, he didn't know. All he knew was he couldn't stand in that alley with her—torn between wanting to wring her damn neck or taking what she was offering him, whatever in hell it was. Because even while he was consumed with a deep resentment that she was back causing chaos all over again, he wanted her, didn't he?

From the second his mouth had met hers, he'd wanted her with such a deep seated hunger that it'd thrown reason right out of his head. And he hated her even more for that. But he still wanted her.

By the time he'd marched his way to St Stephen's Green he was in need of a stiff drink. Not that he'd ever been the kind of man to fall into the bottle to numb everything out. But one drink might help to burn away the anger he felt, and maybe sear his thoughts into better shape. So one drink, and if that didn't help dissipate his anger enough for clear thought then he'd find one of his demolition sites to vent on.

So he walked into the first bar he found off Grafton Street, made a space at one end and dug his wallet out of his pocket while the barman held a glass below an amber-filled bottle. He was staring into the liquid when a voice sounded beside him.

'Penny for them.'

His eye's widened a little. 'Merrow.'

When he glanced round the room she smiled. 'No, no Alex. I'm out with the musketeers.'

She laughed musically when he lifted his brows in question. 'It's what Alex calls my friends. There's four of them, you see.'

Gabe's mouth quirked as he looked back into his glass. 'Yep, sounds like the kind of dumb thing the squirt would come out with all right.'

'He's at home if you need someone to keep you and the glass company.'

The thought of running over to discuss his Ash problems with her brother made Gabe wince inwardly. 'Nah, we're good, thanks.' He tried to dilute the dull tone to his voice by flashing her one of his patented killer smiles. 'Take it you two are okay now, then?'

She grinned. 'Yuh-huh.'

He looked back at his glass, swirling the contents until he'd created a miniature whirlpool to sip from, the liquid burning down his throat and warming his chest. Barring the intrusion, this had been one of his better ideas of late, he felt, even if it technically meant Ash had driven him to drink.

'Girl trouble?'

He laughed. She had *no idea*. Ash was trouble on a whole other level hitherto unknown to mankind. She was a tiny splinter of wood he couldn't get out from under his skin, an itch he couldn't reach, a goddamned stitch in his side that wouldn't go away no matter how much of a rest he gave himself from her.

Even with an expensive Scotch on his tongue he could still taste her and when he turned the glass to let the light hit the liquid he could see hints of the gold in her eyes.

'If it's not I have three single friends over there just *dying* to meet you...'

Gabe glanced over his shoulder and found a table full of women looking his way, one even waved. But he didn't move off his stool, and the fact he didn't put a knowing smile on Merrow's face.

'Yeah, that's what I thought.'

He really wasn't in the mood for this. 'Look, Merrow, I appreciate—'

'But you're not looking for a therapy session.'

'Not so much.' He flashed another smile at her. 'Thanks, though—enjoy your night.'

'I will. Take care, Gabe.'

He held the smile until she left, but it took an effort. And if he'd had any sense he'd have just gone right on over and met all her single friends. But he couldn't, could he? Not 'til he had Ash out of his damn system. Not 'til he could forget how she'd leaned into the kiss when he'd been sure she was about to throw in his face the fact he'd dared to do it—again—when he'd been about to tell her in no uncertain terms that he hadn't been the only one doing the kissing—*again*. She'd leaned in and taken it up a notch, hadn't she? Had moaned when he'd put his hands on her soft skin, wouldn't have stopped him if he'd slid them up over her lithe body, if he'd moved them round and sought out her breasts; filling his hands the way he'd been thinking about filling them ever since she'd started doing that poker celebration of hers.

Pushing the glass away, he lifted his head and studied his reflection in a mirror behind the bar, his mind focussing on the words she'd thrown at him.

But you can't take revenge even if a part of you really wants to because you remember when we were close, don't you?

Yes, he remembered. But then didn't have anything to do with now, did it? She still didn't get it. She still thought she had the upper hand on him, didn't she? Well, the hell she did.

Beckoning the barman over, he threw enough notes down to make sure Merrow and her friends enjoyed the rest of their night before pushing back his stool and leaving in search of a taxi.

He was going to call her bluff.

CHAPTER SEVEN

'WHAT are you doing here?'

Gabe pushed off Ash's door post, walking uninvited into her minuscule living room with a scowl and a waft of what smelled distinctly like alcohol. 'I'd have opened the conversation with "nice place you've got here", but it's safe to say that'd be the lie of the year.'

'Tell me you haven't come over here *drunk*!'

Had he left her and downed a bottle of something before deciding to hunt her down to start yet another argument? Granted, he wasn't swaying on his feet or slurring his words, but even so…

She let the door slam shut, stepping closer, leaning up on tiptoe to sniff loudly before leaning back on her heels and glaring up at him. 'How much have you had?'

Gabe had the gall to chuckle below his breath. 'I'm not drunk. Though it's interesting that's what you thought it would take for me to come talk to you about that little offer you made in the alley.'

Ash's eye's widened, her heart missing a beat. 'You're not serious.'

'Were *you*?'

And she'd honestly thought he'd done a good job of making

her hate him *before*! The urge to slap him was so strong that her palms itched, her fingers curling in against them, nails pressing into the soft flesh to distract her from the sudden pain in her chest.

It was her own damn fault for letting herself believe he might *care*. And for letting that belief carry her back to the depressing place she called home with a lighter step than she'd had since she'd moved in.

'Get out, Gabe.' She stepped back and yanked the door open. '*Right now.*'

He merely folded his arms across his chest, the leather of his jacket creaking. 'Why exactly are you living in a dump like this?'

'Not that it's any of your business, but it's what I can afford. If I'd won the lotto it wouldn't even have made the short list. And it's not a dump; it's *quirky*. Now are you leaving or am I screaming?'

'I doubt anyone would hear you screaming over the party that's starting three doors up—or care enough to come see what's happening with the group of teenagers checking out your neighbours' cars up the street. What do you mean it's all you can afford? Didn't your family—?'

'I pay my own way. My family has nothing to do with it.' She leaned towards the kitchen counter and reached for her mobile, waving it back and forth at him. 'And I can still call the gards and scream down the phone.'

His eyes narrowed, mouth pursing in thought as he slowly turned on his heel and took in the rest of the room with its nineteen-seventies-patterned wallpaper and the well-worn brown sofa she'd attempted to disguise with a throw rug.

'Where's Moggie?'

'In the two square feet out back my landlord imaginatively described as a garden, which is why I *took* this place.' She flipped the phone open, quirking her eyebrows at him as she punched in a number. 'You have sixty seconds. And then I'm screaming so loud down this phone they'll think you're an axe-murderer.'

'Ask for Sergeant O'Brien. His eldest daughter bought a house in one of our new developments a couple of weeks ago—he's a good guy.' He unfolded his arms and walked to the back door, where Moggie greeted him like a long lost relative. 'Hey, pal, how you doin'? What sort of an awful place has she made you live in, huh? Any wonder you chew the furniture when she's out. I'd do more than chew it in protest if I were you...'

Ash genuinely *did* feel like screaming, her hand still on the open door as she flipped the phone shut. So she attempted the old 'count to ten' trick. 'Tell me you didn't drive here.'

His sideways scowl said it all, so she shrugged. 'Well, I wouldn't know *what* you'd do, would I?'

And she wasn't kidding about that.

When he smiled smugly before ruffling Moggie's ears some more she felt the need to slap him again. 'Your owner really does think I'm bad enough to live in this neighbourhood, doesn't she? Yes, she does.'

'How did you know my address?'

'It's on your invoices. I have a good memory for details—as *you* well know.'

Raised voices sounded from next door, got louder as they got closer, and were enough of an incentive for Ash to close the door and scowl harder at Gabe. 'So you thought you'd just down a quick one before you hopped over here for some of that good old revenge sex to complete your evening? Must have been slim pickings at the bar you found.'

He'd lifted up to his full height at the sound of the voices outside, his size now dominating the small room and making Ash feel vaguely threatened. Surely he couldn't have come over for that reason? If he had then whatever was once between them was well and truly gone.

She tried to remember if what she'd said had given him the impression she was serious. Dear Lord—had it? Did he really think she'd offered herself up to be used? Was that what she'd done? She didn't think that was what she'd done. But then she'd said a lot in the heat of the moment, hadn't she?

While the voices faded into the distance he frowned at the door. But when they were gone he looked back at her face, his eyes narrowing until he shocked her to the soles of her feet by ordering in a deep rumble, 'Go pack a bag.'

'What?'

'You heard me. Get whatever you need for the weekend to begin with. And Moggie's stuff.'

'I'm not going anywhere with you.'

'Well, you're sure as hell not staying here.' He threw a pointed finger at the door behind her. 'That's a Friday night just getting started out there. And I'll lay odds it's worse on a Saturday, isn't it?'

Well, yes, it was, but that wasn't the point. 'And where exactly is it you think you're taking me to? Some secluded little weekend love-nest?'

The same finger waggled at her in warning. 'It was you brought up the idea of sleeping together, not me. But we can discuss that further at my place.'

'At your—' She was so flabbergasted she could barely find words. Especially when he'd already moved and was looking around. 'You can't think that I—'

'Where're your bags?' He patted his leg and Moggie fell obediently into step beside him. 'We'll find you somewhere else on Monday. I have dozens of places sitting empty and we'll negotiate some on the rent after you explain to me why it is a Fitzgerald is broke. Has Alex seen this place?'

It was as if a runaway train had just walked in her door. Was he planning on setting her up now like some kind of kept woman until he was tired of her? Just because he was still hung up on some old-fashioned notion of class structure did he automatically think that because he had money and he now knew she didn't he could buy her—take his revenge by sleeping with her until the novelty wore off, use the fact that even though they couldn't get on, on any other level barring a physical one, to—?

She shook her head. It was all just too ridiculous. There had been a time when she'd *known* this man, when she'd spent nearly every waking moment in his company, when she'd shared secrets and laughed over the stupidest things. When she'd—

'It has nothing to do with Alex or anyone else! Dammit, Gabe, would you just *stop*—?'

But he was already in the hall, opening doors at random until he found a rucksack and threw it at her. 'That should do.'

It hit her square in the chest, but she let it drop, lifting both her hands to the door posts to block his way back into the kitchen-cum-living room as he walked back towards her, his eyes glinting with determination.

'Just wait one minute, Gabriel Burke. You *cannot* just barge in here and pack me away to your place for a weekend of—'

He stole the rest of her words from her throat and the very air from her lungs with a deep, long-drawn-out kiss, throwing her headlong into the storm all over again. It wasn't fair that he could do that to her!

She attempted to break free. 'You can't—'

'Yes, I can.' He thrust his fingers into her pony-tail and angled her head to kiss her again, but instead of using his strength and force, he used an even deadlier weapon: one that could almost have been misconstrued as *tenderness*.

And she could fight fire with fire but—

The work-roughened tip of his thumb brushed back and forth against the smooth skin on her cheek while he took his time exploring her mouth from edge to edge, as if he'd never kissed her before and was taking the time to learn the shape of her. He kissed her top lip, kissed her bottom lip; let his tongue slide slowly along the gap until she opened up to him and tasted the hint of whisky still left in his mouth. Just the faintest hint so she knew in her mind he hadn't lied about being drunk while she sought out more of the rich taste with the tip of her tongue.

Oh, this really wasn't fair.

When he lifted his head an inch to change the angle, she breathed out the words, 'Gabe, I won't—'

'Yes, you will.' The whispered words tickled against her sensitive lips, and the torture began again. So that she was gripping tight to the wood to stop from swaying into him, or, worse still—reaching for him. Because he couldn't use this power he had over her to bully her into submission; she couldn't let him use the fact that he flipped on a switch inside her body to control her; she couldn't—

She couldn't stop herself from reaching for him.

And the second her fingers wrapped around the edge of his jacket, he stepped forwards, deepening the kiss as he pushed her round until she was pressed against the kitchen counter, her free hand still attached to the doorway while his tongue tangled with hers.

Well, she'd certainly been right about the theory of stopping angry words by—

He trailed his lips along the line of her jaw, brought his free hand to her waist where he gripped his fingers tight as he leaned his hips in to hold her in place, words rumbling against the sensitive skin below her ear.

'You're right—this is much better than arguing.'

'Gabe—' His name morphed into a moan as his tongue swept against her beating pulse. How was she supposed to string a coherent thought together when he was doing that? Or when—heaven help her—his fingers were pushing the edge of her blouse out of the way so he could run his knuckles across her stomach just above the waist of her jeans, forcing her to suck in her trembling muscles to try and stop the wave of longing from gathering in a tight knot in her abdomen.

She could hear the storm's wind roaring in her ears, the force of it buffeting against her chest so she could barely breathe. And her hand was off the door and in his hair before she'd even realized she'd moved it.

'I can't leave you here, Ash.'

Her heart skipped at the huskily whispered words close to her ear, his knuckles grazing back and forth and upwards. *He cared?*

'Couldn't leave *the dog* here…'

Damn him! She opened her eyes with an angry scowl on her face; jerked upright, pushing against him. And he chuckled against her ear before pinning her back in place with his pelvis, widening his feet so his huge body surrounded her.

'You hate me, don't you?'

'Yes, I *do*!'

His head rose above her face again, angled, lowered, his voice grumbling out the demand, 'Show me how much.'

Ash caught a fistful of his hair in her hand, but she didn't try to hold him back from kissing her again—instead she did exactly what he'd just told her to do, even though she hated him all the more for it. She poured all of the passion of that emotion into the kiss, moved her mouth frantically against his, bit down on his lower lip and then sucked it into her mouth to lick it with the tip of her tongue.

Damn him for making her want him this much; for making

her crave the storm when she'd spent so many years battling to make it through to brighter skies.

He released her head and used both hands on her waist to lift her as if she weighed nothing, tossing her unceremoniously onto the counter-top. But still she didn't try to stop him; she didn't stop him when those same hands dropped to her knees to force them apart so he could step closer, didn't stop the urge to lift her legs and lock her ankles behind his knees.

But when his large hands then rose to cup her breasts she did stop kissing him. Because she had to gasp for air, had to let out the moan from low in her throat, had to hide her face against his shoulder and breathe the scent of leather until she could string a sentence together.

'I don't want you.'

'I don't want you either.'

She swallowed the hard lump in her throat as his hands moved, gently learning the shape of her beneath her bra, his thumbs brushing against the overly sensitive nipples that burgeoned to life with his touch.

'You don't need this.'

'No.' She gasped as he pushed the hard ridge behind the zipper of his jeans in against the apex of her thighs, rubbing the seams of her jeans enough to have her writhe against him before she lifted her face from his shoulder, the tip of her nose close to his, her gaze fixed on his hooded eyes. 'And neither do you.'

He smiled a slow, sexual smile at her as he shook his head, nudging his nose off hers as he held her gaze and said, 'Pack a bag.'

When he tried to find her mouth she moved out of the way. 'No.'

'Yes.' He tried again, she avoided him again.

'*No.*' She avoided him for a third time, fighting the urge to initiate the kiss herself.

When she lowered her lashes to focus her gaze on his mouth, he smiled another one of those seductive smiles he did so well.

'Then we'll both stay right here.'

Her gaze shot back up to lock with his, she watched the blue deepen another shade as he watched the reaction in her eyes while continuing to move his hands over her breasts. He was bullying her—yes. She was letting him—yes, dammit, she was. But somehow that gentle touch against her breasts was doing more than just affecting her body.

He was making her ache again.

She'd never in her life wanted a man more, needed a man more. And the fact that it was *Gabe*; the Gabe she'd walked away from, the Gabe whose friendship had once meant more than she could ever have begun to tell him, the Gabe she'd intentionally hurt when he'd changed that friendship for ever—

He'd told her she'd never win a battle with him. Maybe in order to win the war she needed to surrender to what had probably been inevitable a decade ago?

He leaned in and she let him brush his mouth over hers, his gaze still fixed on hers as he lifted his hands from her breasts and began slowly releasing the buttons on her blouse.

'Let's see what else you don't like me doing.'

That was the thing, though—there wasn't anything he was doing she didn't like, or want more of. Dammit. The brief brushes of his mouth over hers just made her lean in for more of the same; the back of his fingers brushing her skin as he undid each button made her want his hands on her again. And soon she was squirming on the counter and moving her hands to, at the very least, try to get his damn jacket off.

When the last button was undone he lifted his hands to seek hers, moving her arms out to her sides and setting her palms flat on the Formica with his larger hands on top to pin them there before he lowered his head to the hollow between her neck and her shoulder. He then began to blaze a trail of heated kisses across her collar-bone to the hollow on the other side, nudging the edges of her blouse out of the way with his chin so that her skin was grazed by a coarse hint of stubble.

She bent her head back, arched her back up as if showing him she wanted him to keep kissing downwards. But he took the taut line of her neck as an invitation to go back up, earning a low moan of frustration from Ash along the way.

His lips curled into a smile against the skin below her ear. 'You want me to stop, don't you?'

Ash gritted her teeth, fully aware of the reverse-meaning game they were playing. 'So much.'

'Mmm.' The reply vibrated her skin. 'I can tell.'

So he kissed back down her neck, sliding her hands back so she arched her back more, breasts lifting towards his head as he kissed along her collar-bone again until he got to the inward dip at the base of her throat and flicked the tip of his tongue out.

Ash slid her locked ankles up the back of his legs, flexing her thighs so he was held tighter between her knees. And Gabe moved in reply, sliding metal zipper against denim seams in a slow rhythm that made her breath catch and her hips jerk.

Her fingers flexed upwards underneath his. 'Yes...you should definitely...stop...soon...'

When he kissed his way along the lace edge of her bra she felt the impact of it travel like an electric current along her nerve endings to her most sensitive place, which pulsed in response. And when his mouth closed over an aching nipple and suckled through the material until it was soaked a high-voltage charge travelled straight to her very core, deep inside, which caused her abdomen to convulse.

He was killing her slowly. Oh, so very slowly. Her head was spinning and no amount of short, gasping breaths could get enough oxygen to satisfy her thundering heart. There was no way in hell she could fight this, was there?

Gabe lifted his head and studied her face, his eyes so very dark they didn't even look blue any more. 'Tell me how much you don't want me, Ash.'

She had to clear her throat before she told him in a husky voice, 'I won't beg, if that's what you want.'

He smiled. 'You won't say please?'

'No.'

Long fingers closed around hers, lifting her hands to place them around his neck before he wrapped his arms around her waist and lifted her off the counter, stealing her breath again with a kiss filled with soul-destroying passion as he carried her down the hall.

'Yes, you will.' He said the words against her mouth as he shifted her weight up enough to release an arm and open the last door down the hall—the one door he hadn't opened earlier. 'I promise you will.'

Knees leaning on the edge of the bed, he lowered her down onto the covers, his upper body following. He then let go of her long enough to yank his jacket off and toss it across the room while Ash's hands moved from his neck to help him haul his sweater over his head, tousling his hair even more.

Her eyes drank in the sight of him, all taut skin over muscle, the rise and fall of his wide chest showing her how what he was doing to her was affecting him. She set her palm against his heart and felt the rapid thudding, a smile forming on her mouth that she'd done that, even without putting any great effort into it.

Yet.

Gabe lifted her up enough to get rid of her loose blouse,

deftly unclipping her bra and sliding it off her shoulders before he lowered her and kissed his way down until he had her nipple in his mouth again—with nothing in the way. Ash dropped her chin and watched her fingers lift to tangle in the mop of dark hair above her breast, cradling his head in her palm as she felt his tongue flicker out to taunt her.

Oh, dear Lord, how was he able to do that and make it feel so much better than it had ever felt before?

His hands smoothed down her sides as he arched his back upwards to make room for them to get into the button on the waistband of her jeans. Lifting his head, he flashed a smile before moving over to her other breast. And Ash was mesmerized. If it hadn't been for the fact that every muscle in her body was trembling with anticipation and she was painfully knotted up deep inside with an aching that only he could fix, it would almost have felt like an out-of-body experience.

Gabe was making love to her. *Gabe.*

He spent what felt like for ever bestowing worship on her breasts while he freed the button and slid the zip down, his fingers then sliding both her jeans and panties down in one move.

And Ash didn't stop to think about not lifting her hips up to help him, because she'd already said yes to what was about to happen—wordlessly, but they both knew she'd said it.

A whisper of cool air brushed over her heated skin when he moved back to slide the material down her thighs, over her knees, his fingertips tracing the outer edge of her legs. Then she felt rather than saw his gaze rise to look at her naked body in the dim light from the hallway. And she could feel it everywhere it touched, as if he'd put his hands there.

Her arms rose, wrists turning, hands reaching out, and even though she still didn't say the words—he knew. He leaned down and let her hands skim over his shoulders, he dropped his large hands to her waist and lifted her further up the bed, kicking his shoes off before he stretched out beside her and began trailing his fingers from her shoulder to her hip.

'Soft.' The word was barely a whisper as he moved his mouth to her throat and began trailing back down her body again. 'You're so damn soft.'

Ash was shaking, not cold, not nervous; just unable to stop shaking. 'Tell me you brought something.'

She didn't have to spell it out, but his head rose, his face hovering over hers in a myriad shadows and highlighted hints of the features she'd known her whole life.

'You don't have any here?'

She shook her head against the covers, her hips lifting as he trailed his hand down her thigh to the sensitive skin behind her knee. 'Haven't had any…reason to in…a long while.'

'How long?' The question was a husky rumble above her face.

'A-long-while.' She gritted her teeth and felt a moan escape regardless, his fingertips bending her knees and now skimming up the inside of her leg. *'Gabe—'*

He lowered his head and kissed her with another of the soul-destroying kisses he did best, his fingers hovering over the juncture of her thighs as he kissed across her jaw to her ear. 'At *my place*, I have enough for us to do this all weekend. But someone wouldn't pack a bag, would they?'

Meaning he didn't have—?

She groaned in agony and he chuckled into her ear in reply. Taking some time to nip his way back down her neck, he then informed her, 'I didn't come here to make love with you…'

He didn't? What did he mean he didn't? Then why were they—?

He slid his fingers back down her inner thigh, forcing her to writhe in dismay at the loss of the touch she'd wanted so badly. 'Gabe, pl—'

She almost said it.

'I was gonna call your bluff, make you chicken out.' He ran the tip of his tongue over her collar-bone. 'I was gonna prove you never meant what you were offering me in the alley—that you'd say anything to try and win a battle with me...'

Ash froze, her heart imploding in her chest. He'd come to humiliate her, hadn't he? And he'd succeeded. He'd wanted revenge for how she'd made him feel that day. And now he'd got it.

CHAPTER EIGHT

How could he? How could he?

Gabe lifted his head when she remained still, his mouth hovering over her lips again. 'But you've always been dangerous, haven't you, Ash? And now I can't seem to stop. So this is your fault.'

Ash swallowed down the lump of emotion in her throat when he said the husky words with an edge of frustration in them. He wasn't happy about making the confession, was he? He didn't want to want her.

When she knew she desperately wanted him to. She wanted to be able to make him burn as she did, ache as she did—*need*, as she did.

He pushed her leg wider, the irresistibly seductive edge returning to his voice and melting her bones as his hand moved back up.

'I can't stop touching you and it's your own fault I can't.'

Ash moaned into his mouth when he kissed her with more ferocity than he had since she'd thrown her anger into kissing him. He demanded; she gave everything. He punished her for his weakness; she accepted full responsibility for her crime.

His fingers sought out her core and he found the evidence of how much she wanted him.

Tearing his mouth from hers, he leaned his forehead against her brows, his ragged breathing washing over her cheeks, his voice groaning out, 'Dammit, woman, why couldn't you have just packed a bag?'

Ash laughed softly, but it was part shaky sob, because she wanted what he wanted so badly it killed her. 'I'll just have to be creative then, won't I?'

Gabe briefly closed his eyes, a strangled noise sounding in the base of his throat. 'Not this time. This time you're going to give me something I want more.'

He kissed the question off her lips, moving to prop an elbow so he could rest his head on his hand, his fingers moving through her moist heat in circles, dipping lower, then up, never quite touching where she so wanted to be touched the most. 'This first time I'm gonna watch while you surrender to me.'

Ash didn't know if she could do that. 'I can't—'

Not with him watching her. Not with him knowing how much control he could exert over her. She'd be giving him something of herself from deep inside that could never be taken back and she'd sworn—she'd made a vow—that she'd never let herself get lost again. And that'd been before it was *Gabe*, who took so much from her already simply by being able to do to her body what had never been done.

'You can.' He leaned down and kissed her brows, her closed eyes, the tip of her nose and finally her mouth, his deep voice seduction itself. 'Because you know you want to.'

Hell, yes, she wanted to. Because his fingers were building the pressure deep inside her to the point where she was arching up into his touch, small sounds coming from the base of her throat and echoing in the room, sounding so very far away to her ears.

He slid a finger inside her and kissed her lips when she cried out. He drew the moisture up towards her aching clitoris but moved away just when she thought he would give her what she ached so badly for.

'*Gabe.*' His name was a plea.

'I'm here.' When he held his face above hers she turned hers unwittingly towards the light so that he could see her better. 'Look at me, Ash. Surrender to me.'

He repeated the slide of his finger inside her and then upwards, so slow, so purposefully—and with a gentleness that tore her heart out of her chest. She gasped in a ragged breath, turned her face towards his, and let the words out on an agonized whisper.

'Gabe—*please*—'

It only took the smallest touch, just the right amount of pressure, just the tiniest slide of his fingertip back and forth and she was flung headlong into the abyss—her blood roaring in her ears to drown out the cries that came from deep down inside her. She felt as if she were spinning, falling, as if the pleasure of it would never end. And even when her body had stopped violently convulsing she could feel the ripples of it radiate out over her nerve endings.

And he'd done that with just his *hand*?

She groaned at the thought, suddenly feeling more vulnerable than she ever had before. But again he seemed to know exactly what to do; reaching an arm around her waist to roll her over with him so she was lying along the full length of his body, her breasts crushed against the wall of his hard chest, his arms folding around her so she felt—safe—sheltered from the receding storm.

And as her breathing gradually returned to normal his deep voice sounded from above her head. 'So if I tell you to pack a bag this time will you still say no, or do I need to keep doing this until you say yes?'

She lifted her head to smile down at him and then heard

raised voices from the next flat. Gabe tilted his head back to listen as they got louder, Ash frowning at the wall as they got angrier.

And she was still focussed on it when he asked, 'That happen much, does it?'

Ash nodded. 'We're not the only ones who have a turbulent relationship.'

His hands smoothed along her back. 'I think it's safe to say we've discovered a better way of channelling the energy.'

Something thudded against the wall and Ash grimaced, looking down into Gabe's shadowy face before she wriggled off him. 'Gimme a minute.'

He actually let her go, which surprised her. 'To *pack*? Not a problem.'

Ash flashed an almost shy smile at him as she hauled on her clothes. 'You don't give up, do you?'

He was propped on his elbows behind him. 'Well, it should only take a minute. Underwear is a bit pointless, for starters. In fact, you could skip packing and stay naked all weekend.'

And one weekend would probably be all it would take for him to actually own a part of her soul if she felt as naked as she currently did with her clothes back *on*.

The voices got angrier, the tone more vicious and Ash felt her hands shaking as she zipped up her jeans. 'I'll be back in a minute and we can talk about it.'

Gabe had been allowing his thoughts about what had just happened to hide behind the distraction of watching Ash dress. There was something addictive about being able to look at her so freely, about seeing how vulnerable she seemed to be after what he'd done to her. But it wasn't a sweet-revenge feeling he felt, was it? Male pride, yes—what man wouldn't be proud of making a woman fall apart the way she had? But it was more than that—he'd never had a woman quite so receptive to his touch, especially when she didn't want to be.

Maybe that was it. Maybe it was the fact that he'd got her to want him beyond reason so she ignored every bone in her body telling her to run the hell away—or fight him tooth and nail, which was more likely.

Maybes, he was surrounded by them. Not that any of them were helping him deal with the painful state his own body was still in. Because on the subject of not wanting to be physically receptive to another person…

Somewhere in the middle of the maze of maybes, he noticed she was pushing her feet into shoes. And with a frown it suddenly occurred to him she was planning on going some-where—where that somewhere might be when her gaze flick-ered to the wall above his head and her hands shook as she smoothed her hair.

Oh, he didn't think so.

He swung his legs off the bed. 'You're not going over there, Ash. Forget it.'

'I'm just going to check she's all right.'

Gabe caught her elbow when she turned round. 'No, you're not. You said this happens a lot. Did it blow over before?'

'Yes.' She looked up at him with a frown on her face as the voice levels behind the wall got louder. 'But it was never this bad. I just need to—'

'No.' He said the word firmly, tightening his fingers so she knew he meant it, but then loosening his grip when the light from the hall illuminated the genuine concern on her face.

It knocked him back. She kept on doing that when he least expected her to; as if she was some kind of enigma now. When he'd been so very certain—

'If it's worse than usual then we'll phone the gards and report a domestic.' He squeezed her arm in reassurance before letting go to retrieve his phone from his jacket pocket—which proved a mistake, because by the time his hand touched leather she was off out the door.

'Dammit!'

He used his palm flat against the front door to halt her escape. 'You're not going over there. I'll go.'

'No.' She smiled so he knew she appreciated the offer. 'A man turning up could make it worse for her even if you never made it past the door. And if anything was really wrong then you might feel the need to do something about it—knowing *you*—and then who would the gards be carting away?'

Okay, she had a point.

'Listen.' He placed his hands on her hips and drew her a step closer, feeling a sense of satisfaction when she let him and letting it show by keeping a soothing tone to his voice when he ducked his head down to look into her eyes. 'We'll call the gards and report it and while you pack I'll keep an ear on the row in case it gets any worse. If it does then we'll go check it out together—'cos I'm not the only one who might feel a need to do something, am I?'

The wry smile she gave him said she knew he had a point. But she still took a minute to let it go, the indecision shimmering across her eyes. So he squeezed his fingers tighter and lifted his brows in question.

Until eventually he got a reluctant, 'Okay.'

He nodded. 'Good. Go pack.'

When she didn't move he geared himself up for an argument or more persuasion—the latter most definitely his personal preference. And it wasn't just because he wasn't anywhere near finished with what they'd started, it was also because there was no way in hell he was leaving her in the place she was in when he had the ability to do something about it.

It didn't matter who she was.

But Ash did the unexpected yet again, lifting her palms to his bare chest and leaning up to press her mouth to his before she smiled. 'Thank you.'

Gabe frowned, somewhat uncomfortable with her response. 'Thank me by packing.'

At his place, without the distraction of noisy surroundings, they could spend the weekend making love until the unwanted need he had for her was sated. And maybe he'd find out whether or not all the anomalies he was getting glimpses of were just another of her games or if, against all the odds, she'd somehow actually changed as she'd claimed to have.

Another maybe, but he needed to know, didn't he? Forewarned, as the saying went…

'Feel free to stop laughing any time soon.'

Ash made an attempt at stifling her laughter, but it was a feeble one. 'Well, it's not like you're designed for a small car, is it?'

'If your dumb dog hadn't decided he should sit in the front seat too it might have worked better.'

Moggie was too busy checking out the accommodation to listen to his character being maligned, so Ash pouted on his behalf. 'But he's your *friend* now.'

'I've plenty of friends who don't feel the need to sit in my lap when I barely have room to breathe.' He tossed her bag onto one of the long sofas that edged his living room, leaning back against the door frame to watch as Ash wandered around his home.

He wasn't sure how he felt about that, and frankly it was too late in the night and they'd already packed so much into a few short hours that he was too tired to try and figure it out, so he decided to direct the conversation to what had been bugging him the whole way there.

'You know that car's on its last legs, right?'

She shrugged as she leaned in to study some of the framed photographs on the floor-to-ceiling bookshelves against one wall. 'Got me back from France—it's earned its keep.'

'You can't afford to replace it, can you?'

A glance was jerked his way, just long enough for him to see she wasn't happy with the question. Or was feeling the need to back out of what had, in his opinion, only just got started? The journey over had given her time to think after all. When the burning heat there'd been between them had had time to simmer down some—not that he'd been any less aware of the rise and fall of her breasts with every breath she took or the movement of her legs as she changed gear, or the occasional rise of her hand to tuck her hair behind her ear, even with Moggie constantly making the effort to get into his lap.

'We're not going shopping for a car on Monday if that's what you're hinting at. I haven't even said yes to looking at other places to live yet.'

'Oh, you'll be looking at other places to live.' She was a woman living alone in a dodgy area and Moggie was about as much protection as chucking a pillow at someone. 'That part's not negotiable.'

'Just because you now know you have the ability to do all sorts of amazing things to my body doesn't mean you have control over my will, Gabe. Nice picture of you winning something—what is that anyway?'

He liked that she thought he did amazing things to her body and was admitting it out loud without him pressuring it out of her, but he wasn't that easily distracted once he set his mind to something. She should *know* that.

'Businessman of the Year. I'm not kidding about the moving house, Ash. You're not staying there. If Alex knew—'

'I told you it's got nothing to do with my family.' She sighed as she moved onto another set of pictures, and he watched her tucking her hair behind her ear when it was already there. 'And it's got nothing to do with you either. Where I choose to live—'

His sudden burst of laughter brought her gaze to his face from across the room. *'Choose?'*

'Now don't make me come over there and kiss you to stop another argument, Gabe.'

Gabe crossed his ankles before he smiled a slow smile. 'You do what you gotta do—don't let me stop you—but we're still finding you a place to live on Monday morning.'

'No, *we're* not.'

'Yes, *we* are.'

She did that pointless thing with her hand, hair and ear again, frowning as she avoided his steady gaze by looking back at the bookcase. 'No, we're not. If you try to set me up in one of the places you own, even at a reduced rent, it might feel like payment for this weekend, so you can forget it. What's this one with all the kids?'

'What the hell does that mean?'

'It has you surrounded by a bunch of—'

Gabe swore beneath his breath, uncrossing his ankles to push his weight onto his feet and walk across the room to her. 'Not what I meant and you know it.'

Lifting his hand, he curled his fingers round her elbow, frowning down at the distinct tremor he felt as he tugged her round to face him. 'Finding you somewhere else to live has nothing to do with this.'

Still couldn't look him in the eye, could she?

'I can find my own place to live.'

'Yes, you did such a good job of it the first time.'

That earned him a short-lived glare at least.

A part of his brain realized that his fingers were now smoothing against her skin, as if he felt a need to reassure her again.

The simple action earning him a view of the shining hair on the top of head as she studied what he was doing, then an upward glance from beneath long lashes, a small, almost gentle smile on her lips.

She was telling him she appreciated that reassurance, wasn't she? And he remembered a time when she used to smile at him like that—as if she genuinely cared and he wasn't something she'd picked up on her heel.

Amazing what a little dose of desire could do.

'Okay, it's not the kind of place we grew up in, I'll give you that.'

The words were said with a roll of her eyes, but it was a clever two-pronged attack. Because in one sentence she'd not only surprised him by backing down again, she'd also reminded him of the time when they'd been closer, when things had been so much simpler.

But instead of telling her he knew what she was doing he nodded his head, just the one time. 'Right, that's settled, then.'

'No, it's not.' Ash looked almost pained that she had to disagree with him, her tone determined but soft. 'I appreciate that you don't want—' she smiled again '—*Moggie* living there. But I can't be in your debt. Not after this weekend.'

Gabe needed to know. 'Has something changed between your place and here?'

Again the hand-to-ear pointless hair move and the avoiding looking at him, her gaze now fixed on the base of his throat.

'I knew what I was doing when I packed a bag. I just don't want you to think—'

'That you're selling your soul in some way?'

She swallowed hard. 'I'm just saying—'

All right, so he probably hadn't helped anything with the forming of that opinion, but the fact she might genuinely believe his mind worked that way bugged the hell out of Gabe.

'That you think it's what *I* think? I made that offer to find you somewhere else to live before we did what we did, if you remember—it has nothing to do with this.'

Because even his great plan to call her bluff and win the latest round of their battle of wills had changed once he'd got to her place, hadn't it?

When he let go of her arm both her hands grasped hold of his wrists. *'Don't.'*

It was an echo from the alleyway, when she'd leaned in and reached for him. And he knew now that the word was a plea rather than a rejection, didn't he? It made him rack his brain to try and remember if he'd said something in the heat of the moment to make her think she was making a deal with the devil by giving into him. He might well have, because she'd always had the ability to draw harsher words from him than he'd ever used on anyone else.

But then considering what he'd originally planned when he'd gone to see her, she might not have been wrong about the 'dealing with the devil' part. And for some reason that just made him feel—*low*—so he frowned hard and immediately tried to turn it back on her.

'Maybe you're worried because selling your soul is how having sex with me makes you feel?' Another goddamned maybe and Gabe hated her all over again for making him need to know she didn't feel that way. As if he had to have her say out loud that she'd wanted him beyond reasoning or lucid thought.

'Are you asking me if I really do feel I have to sell my body to you this weekend to make things right?'

The very fact she'd known exactly what he was asking gave him his answer, didn't it?

'How many times do I have to tell you the past can't be changed?'

He hadn't raised his voice, but the deathly calm edge was apparently enough to make her grip his wrists tighter, her voice firm as she replied, 'You think I don't *know* that? No matter how many things I might *want* to change?'

The words made him frown all the harder. 'Then what in hell is it you *do* want, Ash?'

The gold flecks in her hazel eyes clouded over, she took a deep shaking breath, but in the end all she did was shake her head. And he knew she still didn't know.

But then who was he to judge her for that? Less than a few hours ago he'd planned to make her ache for him. To make her ache the way she'd once made him ache so he could walk away and let her feel how he'd felt. He'd been thinking of payback, even then, as he had from the moment she'd walked into that party looking the way she did after eight years away.

But the plan had gone awry when he'd taken one look at where she lived and immediately felt a pre-programmed need to rescue her. And when kissing her the way he had had been instinctual rather than premeditated—just as it'd been the very first time he kissed her.

He *had* made her ache, he knew from the way she'd responded when he'd kissed her, when he'd had his hands and his mouth on her. But by the time he'd let it go that far he'd also known the walking away part of the plan just wasn't happening. He'd wanted her—plain and simple—beyond reasoning or lucid thought.

He'd wanted her and she'd wanted him. Hell, even now he still wanted her. But while she was looking at him the way she was, with uncertainty in her eyes and an almost silent plea for him to skirt the bigger issues by hiding them behind passion the way they already had…

Frown fading, he twisted his wrists to tangle their fingers,

squeezing just the once before he let go, his gaze locked on hers
for as long as he could manage to hold it.

'It's late. There's a guest room top of the stairs on the left.'

'But—'

'And on Monday we'll find you somewhere new to live. I
won't have you living there when I can do something about it;
it's as simple as that.' He turned and patted his leg. 'C'mon, big
guy—let's show you the garden.'

CHAPTER NINE

ASH tried to sleep, she really did. But it simply wasn't happening, even when she was so very, very tired. And it wasn't anything to do with a lack of the familiar soundtrack of thumping music and loud voices she'd got so used to, or the fact that it was an unfamiliar place or that Moggie just wouldn't settle and kept whining at the door—as if he'd rather be with Gabe.

It was because she had too many thoughts rattling round in her poor head, too many emotions battling inside her chest and because her body just—ached.

They hadn't had a knock-down shouting match—hadn't even raised their voices—so why did it feel so much worse than any of their other confrontations?

When Moggie scratched the door she sighed heavily, throwing off the duvet. 'C'mon, then.'

Light from the approaching dawn streamed in through the windows so she didn't have to turn on a light to see where she was going until she was downstairs, where one very happy dog was then allowed out through the sliding doors she discovered, and Ash got to explore Gabe's world in the silence. She wandered around the kitchen with its large Aga and heavy wooden surfaces, taking in the very male lack of anything purely decorative with a smile before staring in wonder at all the accoutrements that suggested he might actually like to cook.

Well, if he did then he was a better person than she was; anything that microwaved or came pre-prepared was the limit of her culinary expertise. But she could beat him hands down on the purely decorative accessorizing…

Down the hall she found what could have made a great dining room had instead been turned into some kind of games arcade—complete with wide-screen TV, a games console, games that involved shooting things or racing cars and huge comfy leather sofas worn away right on the very edges of the cushions as if he and his friends literally sat 'on the edge of their seats' while wasting hours proving who had the highest testosterone levels.

But it was in the living room she'd spent so brief a time in that she got a better picture of the man Gabe had become since she'd known him. Amongst the surprising number of books, creased at the spines so she knew he'd actually read them all, were dozens of photographs—his life spread out before her eyes.

And it painted quite the picture.

The photo she'd asked about proved to be some kind of Dream Foundation when she was able to read the T-shirts they were all wearing. But it wasn't the fact that he'd obviously used some of his money to give to the charity or that the kids were hanging off his neck and his legs while his face was lit up, hinting at the kind of laughter she liked best. Nope, it wasn't that.

The photo next to it saw him on a building site, dressed in work clothes and a hard hat in a row of men dressed the same way. But it wasn't the fact he looked so young in it so she knew instinctively it was taken way back at the start of his career, at the time when she'd still been partying and getting into trouble. It wasn't that either.

And it wasn't even the glaring lack of any from his childhood, when she'd been as big a part of his life, if not bigger, than any of the other people pictured in the following years—or the presence of Alex in so many when Ash had given up her right to be there.

No, it was the gradual realization that she'd missed out on so much that heralded the beginning of her slide into real heartache. Because in the pictures, and in the house she was walking through, there was all the evidence of a pretty amazing guy—who'd worked hard to be successful, who'd played hard along the way, but who had done considerate things for others and stayed faithful to those who stood by him and—

Well, looking at herself through the eyes of that kind of man she could understand why he'd had so little respect for the woman he thought she still was.

She switched off the lights in each room and in the hall and wandered back to the kitchen, the ache heavier inside her. A voice in her head telling her she was a lesser person, lacking in something, that she deserved to be treated the way he'd treated her because of the waste of space she'd been for so long.

It had been inside her head for a long time, that voice. And she'd gone through a lot to silence it; had taught herself to lift her chin and dust herself off and get on with her life.

She opened the doors and walked out into the garden as silver fingers of light appeared on the horizon. Rolling her eyes at the fact Gabe's house had the most amazing view from its position overlooking Killiney Bay—because of course it would, wouldn't it?

But when she'd walked barefoot over the dew-soaked lawn, looked at the ivy-covered two-storey house, then wandered back to a stone bench at the end of the patio between the conservatory and the sliding doors, she couldn't stop the heaviness she felt from moving up into her throat, or moisture from welling in her eyes while she watched Moggie bounding around the huge garden with glee written all over his face.

She didn't get it.

Gabe wanted to help her out with living space—he'd protected her by stopping her from walking into 'danger'—he'd been considerate about making sure the woman next door was all right. Had he done all those things because it was just the kind of guy he was? It wasn't because he cared that much about *her*, was it?

But he'd done things to her body that had never been done in any of the relationships she'd ever been in, showing her she'd never had a considerate enough partner before—one who took the time to find out what she was capable of feeling. Why had he been like that if he didn't care?

And he'd made her feel vulnerable, raw emotionally and not used it to humiliate her or gloat over having bent her to his will. Why hadn't he?

She just didn't get it. But what really sent her over the edge wasn't those million and one things she'd thought about inside or the questions she couldn't answer outside—it was that he'd put her in the spare room, because he hadn't wanted her once he'd had time to think about it.

And she wanted him to want her the way she wanted him. She really did.

Gabe stood scowling in the doorway. He could see Ash on the bench, sitting sideways, bare feet flat on the stone, legs bent and arms wrapped around them. She had her head resting on top of her knees with her face turned away from him, but he could hear her—quietly sobbing.

He swore beneath his breath.

Turning on his heel, he marched out of the kitchen and down the hall. Well, she needn't worry, he was done with her. He wasn't so damn desperate he had to pressure a woman into sleeping with him.

He stopped dead. And for a full thirty seconds he stood still, fighting the urge to go out and tell her all that. For another thirty he considered *showing* her how he'd made her feel to prove another point. And then finally, he started to wonder if it maybe wasn't anything to do with him at all. Maybe it was something else, linked to the fact that she was broke and had to live where she was? Maybe she—

Gabe had had a bellyful of maybes.

Ash's breath caught when something slid over her shoulders and Gabe's deep voice sounded gruffly above her head. Oh, no.

Oh, no. Please, please don't have let him heard.

'You'll get cold out here.'

She unwrapped her arms and used one hand to draw the edges of the fleece blanket closer, the other swiping at her cheeks as she forced out a burst of laughter. 'Nah, not me, we Fitzgeralds have the constitution of oxen. But thanks for this. I s'pose you thought you had a burglar, did you?'

'I've been listening to Moggie whine and scratch my paint-work for a couple of hours now.'

'I can touch that up if you have some paint.'

'We both know what happens when I make the mistake of giving you a tin of paint.'

She laughed again, the sound more genuine. 'I promise to behave this time.'

When she didn't look at him he walked to the side of the bench and Ash risked a glance up at his profile while he looked out over the ocean. She saw the tight set of his jaw, saw the wind toss his unruly hair, watched his thick lashes blink a couple of times—and then he shot a sideways glance at her.

'Should I bring out some tissues too?'

She stifled a groan of pure mortification; he *had* heard her. Now how exactly was she supposed to explain this one without completely humiliating herself?

'No, I'm grand.'

'Liar.'

The word was said without a hint of humour or anger, so that Ash was left floundering and squirming inwardly as her mind frantically sought an explanation that would get her out of hot water. PMT might do it…

But Gabe had already taken another breath, one that hinted at impatience before he walked past her and sat on the bench behind her. He didn't make an attempt to touch her, wasn't sitting so close that she could feel his body heat and for a while he just sat there in silence—which pretty much killed Ash.

'Do you want to tell me what's wrong?'

'Honestly?'

'Well, that'd certainly be a leap forward for us, don't you think?'

She had to swallow down a hard lump in her throat before she could answer. 'It would. But I don't think I can just now. It's not your fault, though. I'll be fine.'

It took a long time for him to speak again. 'Is it 'cos of what happened last night?'

'Which part? We managed to pack a lot into one night if you think about it.'

'Yes, but I think you know which part I mean.'

Ash grimaced, angry with herself that her vision was blurring again as she focussed on the brightening sky above her head. And she hated that she was about to lie to him when he wanted honesty from her. But what else could she do?

'It's not because of that.'

'I'm glad to hear it, 'cos I was fairly sure you enjoyed what we did.'

The bitterness in his voice brought her head up. Oh, surely he couldn't think——?

'How can you think for one second that I didn't? Don't you have *ears*? We were lucky my neighbours were too busy trying to kill each other or they might have been the ones phoning the gards instead of—'

The words ended on a gasp when she felt herself being hauled back onto his lap, his arms closing round her body and holding her tight against his before he tucked her head beneath his chin and said a husky-edged, *'Good.'*

Ash allowed herself to snuggle tighter against him, drawing her knees back up and turning into the warmth of his body. *'Idiot.'*

Gabe took a long, deep breath—the movement lifting her up and then down, where she felt the rumble of his voice deep in his chest. 'So this is something else.'

She nodded the half a lie.

'Okay.'

Morning birdsong filled the silence while he held her, his heartbeat steady below her ear, his breath moving the hair against her forehead. And it hurt being held. It hurt that he was being so considerate again. *It hurt, dammit!* And she hated him for it.

His breathing stilled when she shuddered, so she turned into him a little more and touched the tip of her nose against his neck, debating whether or not to take a chance and see if she could turn him on the way he had her. After all—he'd been more than a little turned on before they got to his house, hadn't he? Maybe if she reminded him of that he'd forget who she was again.

So she tentatively touched her lips to his skin.

And felt him let out the breath he'd been holding. *'Ash—'*

She did it again, allowing her tongue to flick out so she could taste the vague hint of salt and pure Gabe, feeling her confidence rise when his body went taut against hers. So she moved enough to untangle her arms and smooth her palms up his chest, over his wide shoulders, tilting her head back so she could kiss the tense line of his jaw.

He growled a low warning down at her. 'Ash, if you keep doing that—'

'Yes?' She moved one hand up into his gorgeously tousled hair, the other framing the side of his face, thumb tracing the indentation where she knew his dimple hid before touching the corner of his mouth at the exact moment his lips moved.

'I won't be able to stop.'

The words created a wave of emotion in her chest that had absolutely nothing to do with feeling miserable. So she wriggled up in his lap and framed his face with both hands, looking him straight in the eye as she informed him, 'You really are an idiot. I don't want you to stop. I didn't want to go into the stupid spare room to begin with.'

He frowned, but the way he searched her eyes told her it wasn't in anger. 'I *asked* you what you wanted.'

'You didn't *wait* for an answer.'

'You shook your damn head.'

'It wasn't a no I didn't want you, it was a no I didn't want to answer you. And since when did you ever take no for an answer from me?'

His mouth twitched, 'And since when did you ever keep quiet about what you wanted when you knew what it was you wanted?'

Ash smiled wryly and looked over his right ear as she gave him a little taste of that honesty he'd been looking for. 'Maybe I was afraid to say it.'

Gabe waited until she looked back into his eyes, shaking his head as he spoke. 'That's not the Ashling Fitzgerald I know.'

'*We-ll*, now you see—' she smiled a more open smile at him '—I've been trying to talk to you about that one for weeks now. But you wouldn't listen.'

He opened his mouth to reply but she leaned in and silenced him before he could say something inflammatory, making a thorough job of exploring his lips from edge to edge and humming her approval when he matched her movements and dipped his head to deepen the kiss.

His large hands moved beneath the blanket, searching for the bottom of her T-shirt and sneaking underneath to touch her skin, sliding up her back and over her shoulder blades before he finally moved one hand round to seek out her breast.

Ash pressed into his hand, moaned against his lips, and then wrenched her mouth free to whisper loudly in his ear, '*Please.*'

He kissed the sensitive skin below her ear. 'What is it you want, Ash? Tell me this time. Loud and clear.'

She lifted her head and looked him straight in the eye again, her voice filled with new-found confidence.

'I want *you.*'

The reward was a punishing kiss while he moved his hands and swept her up into his arms, pushing onto his feet, Ash clinging to his neck and laughing softly as he walked them back into the house. 'You can't carry me all the way up the stairs.'

'Like hell I can't.'

And he did, despite the fact that Ash made him stop several times to respond to the kisses and nips and flickers of her tongue against his skin. Yes, it probably took five times longer than it would have taken without the interruptions, but Gabe felt it was worth it. Especially when he had her laid out on his king-sized bed and was hauling his T-shirt over his head as he knelt on the mattress and joined her, reaching out to do the same thing with hers.

When she reached for his sweats, he took her hands and

pinned them above her head, holding them in place with one of his while he kissed his way down her neck to her breasts—his mouth torturing one while his hand ministered to the other.

She twisted her lower body, her voice breathless. 'Much as I—love—what you're—doing…really I—*do*…I'm already—oh—I'm already ready…'

Gabe lifted his head briefly, just long enough to inform her, 'I'll be the judge of that.'

'I want to touch you too.'

'If you touch me I won't last five minutes. And I have every intention of lasting way more than five minutes—trust me.'

The answer lit up her eyes. 'And I've been ready for this since you did what you did to me at my place. You pretty much had me when you said there was enough protection here to do us *all weekend*.'

He caught her taut nipple between his thumb and forefinger, smiling when she moaned and her head fell back against the covers. 'I do. And we're gonna use every single one of them.'

The answer drew another low moan from her lips and Gabe was amazed by how the sound wound him tighter than he already was. But then he'd been hard for her since they'd been at her place, hadn't he? And even the fact that he'd placed her out of harm's way for a few hours hadn't helped—because he'd known she was down the hall from him, in his house, in a bed, with little or no clothing on. His mind might have decided to walk away, but his body hadn't accepted the decision.

It took an immense amount of control to take his time with her, especially when she fought to get her hands free and set them on him. The touches almost tentative to begin with, then growing in confidence as she learned what drew a response from him, what made him try to move out of her way to slow things down, what made him groan in frustration as she tested the limits of his control.

But he knew he was right to hold back for as long as he did when her touches became more frantic. Her body was shaking with need and when he'd removed her loose shorts to reach for her centre, he found her so ready for him that he was no more able to stop himself from taking her than he would be to survive without breathing in and out.

When he rolled away to reach for his nightstand, she came with him, sliding down his body, kissing his chest and lightly nipping his skin as she reached down to slide his sweats off.

With them out of the way she blew a strand of hair out of her face and held her palm out. 'I'll do it.'

Gabe made a tortured sound in the base of his throat at the very thought of her hands on him there. 'Not if you want me inside you, you won't.'

She leaned down, her hair forming a curtain around their faces as she breathed out the word an inch above his mouth. 'Hurry.'

Was there anything sexier in the world than a woman who could make some demands in bed? Gabe didn't think so. But then that probably had as much to do with the woman making the demands.

He let her kiss him while he ripped open the foil, but the second he had it rolled into place he flipped her over, straightening his elbows as he moved between her outstretched legs, Ash bending her knees and forming a cradle for him. And then he waited for a moment, searching her eyes, taking in her flushed cheeks and the lips red and swollen from his kisses. She was beautiful, wasn't she? But then he'd always known that; it shouldn't have been such a surprise to him.

'*Ash.*' He heard her name before he realized he'd said it.

She smiled an amazing, mesmerising smile up at him, her hands lifting to frame his face. '*Yes.*'

When he pushed into her in one long sweep, her back arched

up off the mattress, a long moan escaping her parted lips. And Gabe stilled again, taking in the sensation of her body wrapped tight around his, waiting for her to open the eyes she'd closed so she could see the play of emotions across the hazel-flecked with fiery gold while his heart thundered. Then he moved his hips, sliding back until he'd almost left her, then forwards a little harder—drawing another moan from her.

And still she looked up into his eyes, as if she couldn't stop looking at him or didn't want to.

He was hanging by a thread. 'Ash—'

She smiled the amazing smile again when he frowned, her voice barely above a whisper. *'I know.'*

He moved his hips again, she slid her hands up into his hair, tangling her fingers—and it took every iota of his self-control not to just take what he so badly needed. But he'd always prided himself on being the kind of lover who put his partner first. He wanted it to be more than good for her, wanted her to cry out as she had for him before. He wanted—*give him strength*—to be able to wait until she clamped around him.

'Gabe—'

She said his name like a plea and Gabe felt her tighten, drawing him further in each time he slid forwards. And he groaned low in his throat because hearing her say his name like that pushed him closer.

How many times had he fantasized about making her say his name like that?

He alternated his weight from one hand to another, untangling her fingers from his hair to hold her hands down on the covers—her arms stretched out on either side of her body.

'Gabe.'

Somehow still managing to keep his movements slow—though God alone knew how—he leaned in to kiss her, tangling his tongue with hers while her spine arched up as tight as a bow-string.

When she lifted her legs and wrapped them around his calves, lifting her hips up to meet each thrust, he wrenched his mouth from hers, straightening his arms so he could look down between their bodies; only to frown harder when the sight of them joined so intimately almost broke the thread he was hanging by.

'Gabe?'

He looked back up at her, his fingers flexing round hers as she looked back at him with so much warmth and intensity—and *raw need*—that it floored him.

'Don't hold back.' The words were said on a softly determined tone, her smile a little tremulous. 'I know you're trying to hang on, and I know why, but I don't want you to hold back.'

'*Ash*—' He ground her name out from between clenched teeth, small beads of sweat forming on his forehead as he attempted to keep the slow, sliding rhythm. She didn't know what she was asking for. He was a big guy and—as strong as she was in mind and spirit—the body beneath his was still so very soft and feminine and so much smaller than his.

'I know you won't do anything to hurt me…' She flexed her internal muscles on his next inward slide and he groaned at how good it felt, his eyes closing as he fought his most basic male urges.

'I want you to take me without holding back.' She took a deep shuddering breath and arched up into his body as high as she could go. 'I need you to—so that I know—so that I know I can do to you what you're—doing—to me.'

When he opened his eyes and looked back into hers he was a goner—the rhythm of his hips already speeding up. He tightened his hold on her fingers, straightening his arms until his shoulders ached. He arched his back—and took what she was giving to him with overwhelming faith that he wouldn't hurt her. And even while he let go and made each thrust harder he could feel her clamping around him, could see in her eyes that she was with him all the way.

It sent a wave of something through his body he'd never experienced before. And if he'd been the kind of man who let himself feel fear, he'd probably have been scared by it.

He'd never completely let go with a woman, had never allowed himself to. Control was something he held onto like a shield, that he used in every portion of his life to make sure that everything was the way it should be. He never lost control—he *never*—

'*Yes*—' Her arched back offered her lush breasts up to him, tempting him to lean down and close his mouth over an erect nipple. But it was too late; he could already hear the blood rushing in his ears, could feel the tightening in his groin that preceded release.

'Ash—*I can't*—'

She called out as her orgasm hit, her body jerking while she clamped so tightly around his painfully hard length that he went still.

And his world simply—*fell apart*.

The room filled with the sound of ragged breathing for a long time—how long, he didn't know, his heart still pounding hard against his chest until reality crept in around the fuzzy edges and he suddenly realized he'd collapsed his full weight onto her, his face buried in the crook of her neck.

But when he tried to move she tightened her legs round his. 'No, not yet.'

'I'm too heavy for you.'

She laughed, and the sound vibrated inside her body, wrenching a torturous groan from his lips that simply made her laugh again. 'Yeah, well, you kinda are—but I like it, so don't move yet.'

Letting go of one hand, he turned his head, settling on the pillow beside her so he could see her profile, his fingers pushing the hair off her heated cheek. But when she turned to look at him he didn't have words for her—not one—and he hated that she could steal that from him too. Because she'd need words, even if they couldn't begin to come close to describing what he'd just experienced.

The smile she gave him was warm and soft while he waited for her to say something to put him under pressure to *find* words, the way all women did at some point. She placed her palm against his cheek, thumbnail grazing his lower lip. And then surprised him again by asking in a softly sexy voice, 'How many of those things did you say you had?'

He chuckled before he kissed her. 'I can get more.'

'I think you should get lots more.' She smiled a broad, dimpled smile as he rolled over onto his back, taking her with him. 'Though we might need to take the occasional break to sleep and eat.'

'And then there's the small matter of the rugby match at Lansdowne Road...'

'You'd rather go to a rugby match than do this?'

Hell, no. But he had to try and hang onto some semblance of normality when the world was suddenly so different, didn't he? It was a survival thing.

CHAPTER TEN

GABE won on the rugby issue, but only after they spent the entire morning exploring each other at great length. In fairness, by then Ash did need a break, if nothing else for the sake of her aching body. And considering where she'd lived for the last eight years an Ireland v France match was a win-win scenario for her, especially when added to the number of times she caught Gabe laughing the laugh she liked best when she yelled and bounced up and down like a fool.

He cooked dinner, she teased him about being a girl—he demonstrated he most definitely wasn't on the kitchen table with her. And after they eventually got round to eating they had an early night, well, because they'd had barely any sleep. Not that they slept the whole night either.

After a 'lie-in' on Sunday they walked Moggie on the beach, had lunch in a pub overlooking the bay and came back for an 'afternoon nap…'

It was a magical weekend.

And a big part of her was scared rigid that when it ended they might never get another like it. Because, although they'd barely been able to keep their hands off each other and had laughed and joked and played, it didn't make real life disappear, did it? It didn't take away the underlying problems or disguise the fact that they'd managed to completely avoid anything resembling meaningful conversation.

Ash knew all that, she did, but then she would look at how well they'd got on, how he'd looked as happy as she felt. And she let herself hope.

But it did mean when they were wrapped around each other late Sunday night, her body still buzzing with the after-effects of another languid session of love-making, that she wished Monday morning wouldn't come at all. But then that was fairly usual the world over, wasn't it?

Gabe's large body was tucked along her back, one leg over hers, her head tucked beneath his chin while he swept lazy circling fingertips over her breast.

'Are you coming to the gallery tomorrow?'

'Thought I might make an appearance.' She tangled her fingers with those on the end of the outstretched arm her neck was resting on. 'Still have three more artists whose work I'd like to see around the country, though. I found some great pieces last week in Donegal.'

'That's where you disappeared to.'

'Glad to hear you missed me.'

'Figured you were avoiding me.'

'Well, it was certainly an added bonus—' she smiled when he flexed his long fingers round hers '—but I guess I'll just have to suffer looking at your face again.'

The hypnotic movement continued on her breast and Ash could almost hear the wheels turning in his head, a sense of impending doom running up her spine.

'You need to behave in front of the crew.'

It was starting already. 'I might have been bad in a former life but I did draw the line at having sex in front of an audience.'

'That's good to know—' he softened the words by placing a kiss in her hair '—but that wasn't what I meant. You do this whole sexy, flirty, reach-out-and-touch-me thing all the time, which honestly—knowing how irresistible I am I can't really blame you for—'

Ash jabbed her elbow into him, his deep laughter vibrating against her back.

'I'm not complaining. I'm just saying you can't do it when the crew's around. They have work to do and you're already too much of a distraction for them as it is. You and that poker dance of yours.'

She smiled, still watching their joined fingers flexing in and out. She liked that he might have been irritated by her distracting his crew. 'Careful now, that one might be misconstrued as a little jealousy.'

'Or possibly the need to have them finish one job so they can do another one?'

'I'm sticking with the jealousy option.'

'Whatever makes you happy.'

She lifted his fingers, kissing his knuckles for that one and could almost feel him smiling behind her. Who could really blame her for wanting to hang onto the magic for a little while longer?

'We should talk about Alex too.'

The magic dimmed a little. 'What about Alex?'

'I'd prefer not to have the sex-with-your-sister chat. I've got used to his ugly mug about the place.'

But it wasn't that, was it? Not that she couldn't see that one being an interesting conversation, but put the pieces together and—

'So as of nine a.m. tomorrow morning we go back to hating each other?'

'I didn't say that.'

'But I'm s'posed to pretend nothing happened.'

'It's nobody else's business what we do.'

'So...' she turned her head a little to try and look at him from the corner of her eye, doing her best to keep her tone calm '...it's something to hide from the world.'

Gabe lifted his head so he could examine her face for a moment. 'Are we gearing up to an argument?'

She really didn't want them to be, so she let go of his fingers, turning round in his arms so she could brush her mouth over his. 'We're having secret sex, I get it. Makes it sound kinda—'

The words weren't even said aloud before he frowned. 'And now you're making it sound like something sordid you should be ashamed of.'

And whose idea had it been to hide away in the first place? She opened her mouth to say as much and then clamped it shut, because she really didn't want to start an argument with him. But neither was she having him think for a single second that she was ashamed.

'I don't have a single regret, if that's what you're suggesting. I'm here because I want to be here. And I don't give a stuff if anyone, including you, thinks a Fitzgerald shouldn't—'

He kissed the rest of the words away, fiercely, drawing her in tighter against his body, eventually coming up for air to reply.

'I don't flaunt my private life, that's all. It's nobody else's business—simple as that. That way there's no post-mortem run-down with the entire universe when it's done.'

What he was saying made perfect sense. But he'd just relegated them to a short-lived affair, hadn't he? It took a little more of the magic away, made her want to hold on a little tighter, her hands moving around his waist to do just that.

She initiated the kissing and touching, blocking out the Monday that was sneaking up on them with each tick of the alarm clock on Gabe's nightstand. And she willed the voice in the back of her mind not to say that same ticking was a count-down to the end.

They'd come this far and less than two days ago she wouldn't have believed that much was possible. So she was damn well gonna go right ahead and hope.

But in the morning Gabe was a different man. For starters his day began way earlier than the weekend Gabe's had and he seemed to fall into automatic pilot as he did what he had to do to get out the door.

Until her car not starting held him up.

'I told you that thing was on its last legs.'

'I'm sure a mechanic can come fix it.'

'Not before eight in the morning, he can't.' Gabe frowned in annoyance as he slammed the bonnet down. 'We'll leave the keys under the mat and put Moggie in the kitchen. You can ride in with me and that way we'll get that list of apartments for you to look at before I drop you at the gallery.'

'I still haven't said—'

The glare from his front door cut her off mid-sentence, so she did the mature thing and grumped about it until he reappeared, locked the door and set her car keys under the mat. By the time he'd got to her again she'd decided she didn't like Monday morning Gabe.

'Get in.'

She pursed her lips as she looked up at him, then, 'A "would you mind getting in, Ash?" or even a "please" might make you a little less of a tyrant this morning.'

At least he had the grace to stop to discuss it instead of *putting her* in the truck, which frankly he was capable of doing even if she put up a fight.

'I have a lot to do today.'

'Uh-huh.' She nodded. 'Well, I hope one of the things on your list is to stop and take a chill pill, 'cos frankly, in my humble opinion—Monday-morning Gabe? Not a patch on weekend Gabe. I liked *him* much better.'

Gabe shook his head, folding his arms. 'He liked weekend Ash better than Monday-morning Ash too. Now *please* could you get in the damn truck so I can attempt to fit thirty hours into the next twenty-four?'

Ash lifted her chin and turned round, a smile twitching her lips. 'Well, since you asked so nicely.'

His phone started ringing bang on eight. And Ash watched and listened with fascination as business Gabe kicked into gear, her smile growing. Oh, he was something, wasn't he? She even forgave him for being so brusque at the house when the realization of how busy his day was became clearer by the minute.

Speaker phone was a great source of information.

'Nelson's say the steelwork for Richmond Street will be late by two weeks now.'

'Tell Nelson's that's twice they've been late—three strikes and it won't matter how much they undercut Riordan's by. We've had the heavy-duty crane sat there for almost a week now doing nothing when it could've been somewhere else. Next.'

'Three phoned in sick off the Meadowlands development—flu going round. I've sent two over from Richmond Street since they're twiddling their thumbs and a plasterer from The Pavenham 'cos they're pretty much done there.'

'Good job. The lads make it onto the Dubai flight on time?' Ash watched as Gabe negotiated the traffic while organizing his troops—all over the world apparently.

It was sexy as hell.

'Haven't had any frantic text messages so I assume so and I booked flights home for the crew they're replacing. Back on the twenty-eighth. Oh, and Sean Kenny wants you to check out the access to the office-tower project on Sussex Road while I remember.'

'Today?'

Ash thought it was a bit like discovering a superhero's secret identity or that he led a double life, though she'd bet he'd prefer the first description, given the choice. All the time when he'd been working at the gallery with his crew she'd been vaguely aware his phone rang a lot. His absence she'd definitely noticed—she'd known the minute he left the building or worked only half a day. But it had never occurred to her he had all this other stuff going on in the background.

Yes, because she'd been too busy being fascinated by him in work clothes, hadn't she? Did kind of beg the question of what he was doing at her gallery job in the first place, though, didn't it? If he was so busy and all…

'Yup—he'll be there at twelve.'

Gabe sighed as he made a turn. 'Let him know I'll be there. That the lot?'

'For the next ten minutes it is.'

Throwing a brief half-smile Ash's way, he added, 'Get Fiona in Holdings to run me off a list of apartments—ground floor, two bedroom, garden or near a park if possible—commuting distance to Eden Quay. I'll be there in twenty minutes for them, traffic allowing.'

'Gotcha, boss. Talk to you in ten.'

'Bye, Mick.'

Ash leaned back against the door, folding her arms across her breasts so he knew she was getting serious with him. 'Gabe—I haven't said—'

He held up a finger, which widened her eyes. Had he just *shushed* her? He'd better not have.

'Call Kevin O'Dwyer.'

His all-singing-all-dancing phone did as it was bid so Ash was forced to listen while he arranged to have her car collected, repaired, serviced and the tyres checked. Oh, yeah, and a full valet. It was unbelievable.

'Thanks, Kevin.'

'So what am I having for lunch?'

'What?' He frowned over at her.

'Well, you have the rest of my life organized in three minutes flat so I was just wondering if you'd let me know what I'm eating for lunch today.'

Gabe made the mistake of chuckling and Ash's brows rose. The man genuinely had no idea when he was in trouble, did he?

'Sweet and all as it is what you just did with the car—I could've done it myself, after I'd shopped around for prices. I'd have skipped the valet, mind you. And as to the apartments issue, I'm not joking, Gabe. I haven't decided if I'm moving. I paid three months' rent up front as well as a deposit so if I move it won't be for a while yet.'

There, and she couldn't make it much plainer than that, could she? Plus she'd managed the whole thing without raising her voice, so surely he'd see she wasn't being unreasonable. Still, just to be sure, she unfolded her arms and reached her hand to his arm, squeezing once.

'I do appreciate what you're doing. I just don't need you to. I can stand on my own two feet these days. And I kinda like that I can, y'know?'

He didn't answer for a while, his gaze focussed on the road while she watched him thinking. And she could almost see him doing it now having spent so much time 'getting to know him'.

When he finally glanced over at her as the traffic slowed, he examined her eyes for a second. 'You're really gung-ho on this independence thing, aren't you?'

'Yes, I am.'

'Without any help from your family.'

She grimaced. 'Not unless it's under my own terms.'

'Meaning?'

Now there was a question. And there was no simple answer to it either, not without going into a very long-drawn-out explanation of her past—the very past she was trying not to remind him of too often. Because it was still thin ice for them, wasn't it?

She took a deep breath, exhaling it with puffed cheeks. And she didn't have to say anything before he read the signs.

'I take it there's a lot to that answer?'

'Yes.' She crinkled her nose. 'Kinda is.'

He nodded, turning his attention back to the traffic. 'Okay.'

Now he thought she didn't want to talk to him, didn't he? And she didn't want him to think that, didn't want him to think the fact that he wanted to know didn't matter to her. Unless he really didn't want to know and that was why she'd got the one-word answer?

She'd never been in so complicated a relationship with a man before. It was hard work.

'Independence is about choices, right?'

He nodded again. 'The freedom to make them, yes.'

She waited a minute for it to sink in.

A wry smile was thrown briefly her way. 'All right—I'll back down on the car. But I *was* giving you a list of *choices* for the place to live.'

'Which I *appreciate* but—'

'You're not safe living where you are.'

She smiled a larger smile, loving the fact that he was concerned about her safety. It was an echo of better times again, when she'd always had him there to rely on—no matter how much trouble she got herself into. For a long while he'd been the one solid thing that had kept her safe, held her back from that leap over the edge into oblivion. She didn't think he really understood what a difference it'd made, or the damage he'd done the day he kissed her and gave her a reason to break free...

'I'm careful. And it's not the first rough area I've lived in, trust me.'

'Why?'

'Why trust me?' She tried to laugh it off. 'Now, Gabe, if you start an argument we're not exactly somewhere I can stop it happening, are we?'

He shook his head. 'Don't do that.'

''Cos I might cause an accident...'

'No.' He looked her straight in the eye. 'Don't avoid the question. You either want me to know who Ashling Fitzgerald is now, or you don't.'

Her eyes widened. 'Just like that?'

'Just exactly like that.'

How could he make it sound so simple? Didn't he know what a minefield that one was? Because, yes, she wasn't the person he'd known and disliked so much any more and she loved that he was starting to believe that. But who she was now was indelibly wrapped up in who she'd been before, the new rising up from the ashes of old—*no pun intended*. Ash just didn't know if—

She shook her head.

Gabe caught her doing it, his deep voice holding a faint edge of frustration. 'Is that a no you're not prepared to talk to me or a no to something else? I'm still not too hot on those.'

His phone rang.

So while he dealt with another list of work-related things Ash looked out of the windscreen at the busy Dublin rush-hour traffic. It had been a no she wasn't sure she could take the chance, that was what it'd been. She wasn't sure she could just open up and let it all out when he was such a big part of the beginning of it all. But if she didn't then where did that leave them?

It left one weekend where the world was shut out and they'd got to indulge in the one area where they were completely and utterly compatible. But it wasn't as if that were enough on its own, was it?

And if she opened up she might lose him again.

The phone call ended. But before Gabe had a chance to look at her it rang again, and the frown on his face wasn't anything to do with the conversation he got into about planning permission and zoning and the like. Ash knew it was because the things that had kept them apart before were sitting between them like thick, heavy, oppressive humidity in the air on a summer's day.

She hated it. She hated that it had taken less than an hour to take such a big step backwards. And she hated that the damn aching was back.

The last call ended as they pulled into the reserved parking outside his offices, the intertwined letters of the B.D.L. sign by the door glinting in the sunlight.

Gabe turned the engine off and stared at the sign, trying to decide just how far to push and whether or not he actually wanted to push at all. Meanwhile it occurred to him he was staring at the sign that'd been a source of pride to him for years and he wasn't getting the same kick out of seeing it. It had been the constant interruption of all the phone calls that'd done it.

He'd got frustrated by how much his work was getting in the way, when it was that very element of distraction he'd sought out at the start of his career.

One weekend couldn't have changed him that much. But now the weekend had happened he was going to have to open Pandora's box, wasn't he?

He turned in his seat and found Ash looking out of the side

window, her reflection showing she was chewing on her bottom lip. Almost as if she was nervous.

And since Gabe had already decided to stop playing the maybe game… 'Are you afraid to tell me again?'

She made a small noise that sounded like a grunt of discomfort so he took that as a 'yes' and pushed again.

'What are you worried will happen if you start sharing stuff with me?'

That earned him a glare in the reflection.

'Okay.' He nodded slowly. 'You're worried it'll lead to more arguing and we'll be back where we were before.'

'I hate that you can do that.'

'Do what?'

'Figure me out that easily after one weekend.'

He laughed at that. 'Oh, there's nothing easy about trying to figure you out, Ash, believe me. And I've had way more than one weekend to take a shot at it.'

Reflected Ash frowned briefly at what he'd said, a hand lifting to brush her hair behind her ear. 'Why is it suddenly so important you do?'

Oh, that one was a corker of a question.

Frowning himself, he sighed heavily and looked out of the windscreen again as if an answer would magically appear to lift him out of the danger zone. In the end there was no escaping the damn 'm' word.

'Maybe what I got to see of the new Ash at the weekend is enough to make me want to get to know her better.' He looked back at her reflection. 'I liked the Ash in the beginning years well enough, what I've seen of the one in the here and now hasn't been overly bad—though she could do without those cold feet she brings to bed at night. So it might just be the one in the middle I have the biggest problem with. I'd like to find out.'

'What if they're all the same person?'

That was another corker of a question, one he could only give an honest answer to. 'I don't know.'

The reflected Ash pursed her lips together, swallowed hard and then met his gaze with a very small smile to match her small voice. 'And that right there's pretty much what I'm afraid of.'

Gabe glanced around the crowded street and made a spur-of-the-moment decision, unclipping both their seat belts and pushing his seat back as far as it went before he hauled Ash across onto his lap.

Squashed in tight between the steering wheel and his body left him little room to manoeuvre but somehow he managed to get his arms around her shoulder just before her surprised face leaned back so she could look at him.

'Excuse me—secret affair?'

'Extenuating circumstances.' He placed a swift kiss on her lips. 'Now listen up—'

'You bully me entirely too much, you know.'

'Are we listening or are we making a feeble attempt to get me to drop the subject? 'Cos I think we both know you've known me too long to believe that'll work.'

She scowled at him.

But when she stayed silent he knew he'd won, and when her lashes lowered so her gaze was fixed on the base of his throat he knew she was worried about what was coming, so he kept his voice low and calm.

'You need to know there aren't any guarantees this'll last, Ash. There's too much stacked against it as it is. One weekend doesn't fix everything.'

She nodded. 'I know, and—'

'I'm not done.' He squeezed his arms a little tighter in that reassurance-giving way he seemed to have got into the habit of doing with her of late, which was a little at odds with what he'd already said. So he took a breath to try and sort out his thoughts before he attempted to get out exactly what he *did* mean.

'But the weekend does change it—'cos right now, with you on my lap, all I can think about is finding a bed and spending the rest of the day in it.'

She glanced up and smiled the kind of smile that made his body react as if the idea were an imminent possibility.

'Quit that.'

The smile grew. And Gabe couldn't help but smile back for a second before he continued.

'Much as I'm more than sure we'd enjoy spending every day in bed for the next few weeks until we get tired of each other—it's not gonna happen. 'Cos I have work and you have a gallery to set up. So that means we have to treat this like an actual relationship for a while. And people in relationships spend time getting to know each other.'

He watched as the thoughts moved across her hazel eyes before she spoke. 'And if they get to know each other and don't like what they find then they end it.'

'Yes, they do.'

'But if they already know something they don't like it can cloud their judgment.'

That was true. 'Yes, it can. But if they somewhat miraculously overlooked it long enough to have had that weekend in the first place then they can make an attempt to try the getting-to-know-each-other part. And that's as far as I'm prepared to give in on this so make a decision, Ash.'

The fact that she took so long to think about it made him tell himself what he was attempting was pointless. Less than three days ago he'd have thrown a 'that's what I thought' at her and walked away. But three days ago it hadn't mattered, had it?

Much as he'd have preferred it not to—it did now. He needed to know who she was, how she'd changed, when she'd changed, what had made her change. He didn't know why he needed to know, but he did. That way, whenever what was between them finally fizzled out, he could put his tangled history with her to bed once and for all and be done with it. He could move on.

Ash looked up into his eyes. 'How about we try starting with the more recent, easier stuff and then work our way up to the difficult years?'

'I can work with that.'

'Good. Can we start with the bullying?'

He leaned in to grumble the words against her mouth. 'If I didn't bully you we wouldn't even have got this far and you know it.'

'I still hate you.'

The smile formed against her mouth. 'I know.'

She leaned back a little. 'This sharing stuff is a two-way street, you get that—right?'

'Yes—' he leaned in again '—but if you can do it, I can. Not like I'm likely to let you outdo me, is it?'

'A different battleground…'

She sighed against his mouth a millisecond before he claimed her lips, sealing the deal the best way he could think of. And she was right, it was a different battleground but it was the same damn war, wasn't it?

Only this time he wasn't coming out the loser.

CHAPTER ELEVEN

'UP A little on the left, no, down a bit.'

Gabe looked over his shoulder. 'You know, a spirit level would get us out of here before I turn grey.'

She smiled at him, tilting her head towards her shoulder so her pony-tail flicked outwards and swung while she placed her hands on her hips and crooned at him.

'Poor baby all tired out from hanging the pretty pictures on the wall?'

He looked back at the piece in front of him. 'What exactly is it supposed to be again?'

'That one's called "Melancholy".'

''Cos melancholy is how you'll end up feeling when you realize how much you paid for something a four-year-old could have done?'

Ash stepped up to his side to punch his upper arm, the smile still on her face. 'Funny guy. Still needs a little up on the left. You head-of-the-company types are very bad at *following* instructions, aren't you?'

Turning, he placed his hands on her hips and drew her in against his body, leaning in closer to inform her with the kind of low, rumbling voice that did things for her every damn time, 'Depends what I'm being instructed to do and where and for

how long. I'm very good at things like lower, more, just there—
harder…'

The low words had the same effect they always had, the light
dancing in his eyes doing things to her pulse rate she loved to
have done. Damn, but he was addictive.

'Just keeps on coming back to the bedroom with us, doesn't
it?' Hands resting on his forearms to lean on them, she stood
on tiptoe to kiss him, patting him once with both hands before
she moved away. 'You have a one-track mind.'

'You love that I have a one-track mind.'

That was true. Unfortunately with each week she spent with
him there were a great many things she could add to it. No
matter how many flippant jokes she made to cover it up, a list
was forming. And it was unfortunate because she still felt as if
she was on some kind of ticking countdown clock with him.
The very one that had started ticking that first Sunday night.

Though they'd survived most of the smaller stuff they'd
been working their way through. Like talking about her time
in Paris, after she'd fled the humiliation of having her semi-
naked self plastered all over the newspapers at home, where
she'd discovered a passion for art when she'd wandered into
the Louvre one day. That passion then led her to find a History
of Art course she could afford by supplementing what little
money she had left from her trust fund working in bars and
bistros at night. She'd told him about the friends she'd made,
about the beginnings of her homesickness for Ireland, about the
plans she'd formed for the gallery…

Gabe had listened to it all and asked questions and said
things that let her know he understood and she'd loved that he'd
done that, that he now seemed to know she'd changed in her
time away.

She'd then listened while he talked about building his
company from nothing, with sheer hard graft and bloody-

mindedness to succeed no matter what his start in life might have been. About his first freelance jobs and talking the group of men into joining him to put together his first crew. She'd listened to it all, asking questions and saying things she hoped allowed him to know she understood why he'd maybe been more driven than most to succeed—that she was proud of what he'd built for himself. And she'd loved the smile on his face and the bright light in his eyes that told her he knew she understood, that he didn't need anyone else to feel pride on his behalf but he liked that she did anyway.

Then there were the seemingly insignificant things that helped, like talking about favourite movies and books and debating bigger issues like the economy and politics and the latest world news—a surprising number of which they had similar views on, some which, wonders never ceased, they'd managed to agree to disagree on.

But after a month fitting time together around work and three more wonderful weekends at his house they'd still managed to avoid all the bigger stuff. And it was getting hard to avoid it.

'I'd be able to appreciate your one-track mind if we got the last of these hung up so we could go home.'

She was glad she had her back to him when she referred to his place as 'home'. It had been happening a lot of late, she knew that as well as she knew it was a reflection of how it felt like more of a home to her than she'd had in a long time—but so far she'd got away with it.

And when he didn't comment on it she reckoned she'd got away with it again, so she reached her hand up to move 'Melancholy' the necessary half-inch up on the left-hand side to make it straight.

'Needs a little more up on the left.'

She stepped back a step, frowning in concentration. 'No, it doesn't.'

When she glanced over her shoulder his eyes were sparkling at her and even though he'd managed to accompany it with a completely straight face she knew that sparkle too well not to know she was being had. So she rolled her eyes.

'Oh, for goodness sake—use the damn spirit level if it'll make you happy. What is it they say about boys and their toys?' She lifted her nose in the air to walk past him for the next painting. 'But keep in mind, big guy—leave a mark on anything and you automatically own it.'

She sincerely hoped there wasn't some kind of subliminal message in that one too.

He caught her elbow when she got to his side, swinging her round to face him before folding his arms tightly around her, crushing her against his body and rocking them side to side as he turned them in circles in the general direction she'd been headed.

'First up: not a toy when it's useful—it's a time-saving device so people can leave and make the most of the Friday night when someone has some stupid gallery opening on the Saturday night—messing up a perfectly good *weekend*.'

Ash hooked her thumbs into the belt loops of his jeans and smiled up at him. 'Point taken.'

'See, I love it when you know well enough to give in without a fight.' He chuckled when her mouth dropped open in mock outrage. 'Second thing: if I had to own any of these things they'd never see the light of day again, 'cos, frankly, your idea of what constitutes art—not the same as mine.'

'We just need to brush up on your art appreciation.'

'I'll brush up on my art appreciation if you learn all the finer points of the construction industry.'

She pursed her lips. 'All right, that one we might need to negotiate.'

Gabe stopped circling them and bent her backwards while she laughed, his head descending towards hers. 'I'm all for you trying to persuade me some...'

'Hello, anyone home?'

He let go of her so fast she almost fell over. And she scowled at him in annoyance when he put the safe distance of a couple of feet between them as her brother appeared from underneath the mezzanine stairway. Not just because he'd almost let her fall—but because he was still so damn adamant about no one knowing there was anything going on. Frankly she was getting tired of the secret part of the secret affair.

Her annoyance at Gabe came out in her tone of voice to her brother. 'If you're here for the party—you're a day too early.'

Alex glanced briefly at Gabe, a look of surprise crossing his features before he hoisted forward the long box he'd been carrying underneath one arm. 'Nice to see you too. Merrow sent you pretty dresses to try for the latest round of Fitzgerald social engagements you've been roped into. And speaking of getting roped into...'

Gabe flashed him a smile. 'Hey, you know me—I always see a job all the way through to the bitter end.'

'Control freak.'

'Errand boy.'

Ash scowled at them both and reached for the box. 'While you two see who can spit the furthest I might try and get some actual work done. Tell Merrow I appreciate these, Alex.'

'Will do. Still don't know why you didn't just go hammer Mother's account at Clery's myself—if you're being dragged to all these things to smile your best Fitzgerald smile.' He surrendered the box to her, shot another suspicious glance at Gabe and then began to wander around and look at the pieces on display.

He wasn't going to leave, was he? And Gabe aimed a look of annoyance at Ash as if it were *her* fault. Which she answered with a lift of her brows and a glare that said 'don't you dare blame me'.

'Got your name stamped on anything here yet, Gabe?'

Ash smiled sweetly at Gabe's face. Answer that one then, big guy. And as if her brother were too dumb to know that something had changed when Gabe was with her after hours, alone, and there wasn't a pool of blood anywhere. The way Ash saw it, even if they didn't manage to get through the difficult stuff they hadn't dealt with yet there was no reason to hide any more, was there? They were stronger now, weren't they?

He shook his head. 'Your sister's idea of what art is isn't the same as mine.'

'Yes, we were just discussing that when you came in.' She continued to smile sweetly when Gabe's expression darkened. 'Weren't we?'

Alex continued to wander around while Gabe and Ash faced off in a silent battle of wills. 'Place looks great, though.'

'Thanks.' They answered in unison, Ash stifling laughter that they had while Gabe frowned.

And the fact they did made Alex turn round and stare at them both while crossing his arms, lifting one hand out of the crook of his arm to wave a pointed finger back and forth as his eyes narrowed. 'You two attend a few therapy sessions or something since the last time I saw you? 'Cos this is freaking me out a little bit.'

Ash cocked her head in challenge. 'Gabriel?'

'*Ashling.*' The warning was clear.

Alex stood still for another moment, then stepped forward, bending over at the waist when he was a foot away and freeing his hands to reach out and pat both their arms. 'Well, you kids continue to play nice. Just don't go thinking now you've buried the hatchet that it means you can tag-team against me again.'

He stood tall and waited until they both looked at him before smiling at them each in turn. 'Okay, then, I'll see you tomorrow night.' He jerked a thumb over his shoulder. 'And just so you know—that splattered grey painting is crooked…'

Gabe waited until the door closed before he asked in a calm voice, 'We've decided to go public, have we?'

'Oh, come on.' She placed her hands on her hips and glared at him. 'You think he doesn't have a pretty good idea already?'

'He would've done if he'd stayed five more minutes, wouldn't he? 'Cos you'd either have told him or made us have the kind of argument where he'd have known fine well what's going on.'

'And the world would have ended, would it?'

She watched as he folded his arms and spread his legs wider, fully aware of the fact he was probably gearing up to a full-blown argument—their first in weeks. So she tried a pre-emptive strike.

'Are you worried your professional image might somehow get dented if you're linked with Ireland's former premier wild child? Is that it?'

The question sent a flicker of surprise across the blue of his eyes before he frowned hard. 'Where the hell did that come from?'

'Well, it's not like you're the only one who remembers my sordid history, is it? I've had jibes thrown at me at every social engagement I've been forced to attend as a Fitzgerald since I got home. So maybe now that you're this pillar of the community you don't want to be seen with me?'

'That's the dumbest thing you've ever come out with—which is *saying something*. I told you before my private life is nobody's business but mine.' But the frown had faded some and the flicker of confusion was back in his eyes. 'And what do you mean "forced to attend"? If you don't want to fly the good old Fitzgerald flag then why go?'

'Don't change the subject. If it's not that, then what is it?'

She stood her ground, even though she knew she was rapidly pushing them off the safe stuff and into the region of difficult stuff. But she really was sick of hiding—she was sick of not being able to so much as smile at him the way she felt like smiling when she saw him. Or share a joke when she thought of something she knew he'd laugh that laugh she liked best at. Or lean in to kiss him when he gave her the heated look that always sent her blood running faster through her veins and made her heart do weird skipping things that she hated him for being able to make it do.

No man had ever made her damn heart do that!

Why couldn't she let the world see when she was happy? It'd had a good enough look when she'd been lost and lonely and miserable…

'I told you—it's nobody's—'

'So you've never taken a single woman you've had an affair with out in public without a bag over her head?'

'We're doing the exes conversation now too? Good—that'll help. Shall we start with the bastard who sold pictures you didn't know he'd taken to the papers the second he knew you couldn't fund his party lifestyle for much longer?'

Well, yes, because obviously she'd shared that information with Gabe so he could throw it back at her mid-argument. Ash shook her head, fully aware that he was doing it to deflect her from what she wanted to know. They might have got better at sharing stuff but they'd also got better at recognizing they were each as defensive as the other at times, hadn't they? And knowing that meant they both knew to let some things slide rather than allowing them to fuel the fire.

Looking away from his face, she damped her lips with the tip of her tongue and asked the question that had been plaguing her for weeks.

'It's that you don't see the point, isn't it? 'Cos you know this won't last. So what's the point in the world knowing, right?'

When he didn't answer straight away she felt the ache she was so newly familiar with growing exponentially inside her. It shouldn't hurt so much to have it silently confirmed, should it? Not when they'd only been together for so short a time. It wasn't like a few weeks were anything major when compared to the years they'd spent as two people with so much anger and bitterness between them.

But it did hurt. It hurt just as much as it had the day she'd said the dreadful things she'd known would send him away— her best friend from childhood, the guardian angel who was always but a phone call away when she needed rescuing. She'd looked into his eyes that day and watched hurt morph into anger and hatred. And it had broken her heart so irreparably that it'd been two years before she'd felt anything again; two years of self-punishment to pay for what she'd done.

His fingers curled under her chin, turning her face towards his as he firmly told her, *'Don't.'*

It reminded her of the night in the alley when she'd been unable to stop reaching for him. And just as she had, he reached—the hand on her chin sliding around her neck to draw her closer, his arm snaking around her waist to hold her tight while he lowered his mouth to hers and kissed away any chance of angry words.

Because when they kissed there was no room for anything but the kissing itself, was there? And everything that would follow the kissing when kissing wasn't enough and words couldn't be said because they didn't exist.

She leaned into the hard wall of his chest, her hands rising to frame his face as his warm mouth moved with hers, tenderly; as if he could kiss her for an eternity and never get tired of it. That was how it felt to her when they kissed, in fact they could spend ages on one of the many sofas in his house at the weekend and just kiss. She loved it when they did that. It was on her list.

The ache inside her dulled a little with each sweep of his mouth, with each gentle sucking movement, with the seeking tip of his tongue, but just like always it moved down deeper inside her, tightening into a knot, building tension as it transformed into an ache at her very centre—where she wanted him to be joined to her.

She moaned in frustration, moving back enough to murmur against his lips, 'Take me home.'

His lips moved into a smile. 'Nope.'

Using the arm around her waist, he lifted her feet off the floor, carrying her towards the stairs while he began kissing her again. Then all of a sudden he changed direction, mumbling against her mouth.

'Hang on—need jacket.'

Ash laughed softly, moving her head back a little to look up at his profile as he tried to find where he'd left it. 'What do you need your jacket for?'

'For what's in my wallet—after that first time at your place I swore I was never getting caught short again. It's that boy-scout thing: "be prepared"...'

'Isn't that the girl-guides thing?'

He threw a meaningful smile her way. 'Now we know what happened the last time you tried telling me I was a girl, don't we?'

She bit her bottom lip and smiled mischievously back at him, which earned her a swift, hard kiss. And then, tightening his arm to secure her before he bent over to lift his jacket, he smiled a smile that made her heart do that strange twisting thing again, demanding with an almost husky rumble, 'Hold on tight, then.'

He remembered, didn't he? And the command of old—an echo of their early childhood, when she'd been so determined Gabe should carry her everywhere—just made her heart twist all the harder. She *loved* that he remembered that. So she wrapped her legs around one of his, locked her ankles and answered with the simple answer from those old days, her voice almost husky too.

'*Go.*'

While he attempted to shake his wallet out of his jacket pocket she rained kisses along his jaw and down his neck. Moving to his mouth when he was upright again and her ankles unlocked, she wriggled to get her hands into a position to start undressing him, forcing him to let her body slide down his 'til her feet hit the floor, so he could hold firmly onto his prize and keep kissing her back at the same time.

'Come on.' He untangled her hands, closing one in his and tugging her behind him towards the stairs. 'We're going to christen your gallery. I've had a place in mind for this since we finished the place.'

Lord but she loved how his mind worked. 'Where?'

'Just trust me.'

She jogged round in front of him, walking backwards up the stairs and making it difficult for him to concentrate on keeping his footing by kissing his mouth, nipping playfully and seeking out his tongue as she unbuttoned his shirt and tossed it to one side. When he set her away from him at the top of the stairs to throw cushions off the sofas that lined the walls of the upper level, she cocked her hip to one side, beginning to unbutton her blouse to speed things up.

Gabe turned, his eyes dark as he watched her slow down her striptease, opening the edges of her blouse and running her fingertips over the lace on her breasts while he watched, his voice low.

'Keep going.' His hands dropped to his belt buckle.

So Ash smiled a slow, sensual smile, her eyes on his movements while he watched hers. And she didn't need to look into his eyes to know he was still watching, because she could feel where he looked as she had every day since the time in the hallway of her family's house. He could strip her naked with his eyes and she'd feel it; he could make love to her with his eyes and it would make her knees go weak, and she loved that he could do those things to her.

Her blouse dropped to the floor, hands shaking as she unclasped her bra before shrugging her shoulders and letting it slide down her arms while she walked towards him. He did that to her too, every damn time—made her tremble with need, almost as if she'd fall apart if she didn't have him inside her as soon and as often as humanly possible. How had he done that? she wondered. When had having him as close as it was possible for a man and a woman to be become as important to her as water or food or air?

She sighed when his hands reached out to cradle her breasts, the sigh becoming a series of moans and mumbles of encouragement as he kissed down her neck, over her shoulders and downwards.

'Don't…go…slow…' She made the demand firmly between kisses of her own, dropping her hands to undo her jeans and wiggle out of them before reaching for him again.

Moving his hands long enough to lift her up and lay her out on the cushions, he swiftly returned them to her breasts, his grip tightening, thumbnails teasing her nipples into taut buds. 'Wasn't…planning…on it…'

Shoes were kicked off, hands frantically pushing remaining clothing out the way while they continued to kiss—harder and faster—demanding more from each other's mouths; Ash's curves fitting into the dips and hard planes of his body as if she'd been made for him.

The thought made her heart twist again. So she held him tighter and kissed him harder.

Gabe lifted his head, kissed her hairline, her brows, her closed eyes, her nose—ignoring her swollen lips in favour of blazing a trail down her neck to her breasts, where he took mere seconds to have her moving beneath him and fighting to switch positions so she could follow the same path he had.

But when she kissed down his ribs, over his stomach and lower still, looking up at him with her intentions sparkling in her eyes, he groaned. He leaned up, his hands tightened on her waist, drawing her back up to fuse his mouth with hers while he reached a hand between their bodies to swirl his finger into her moist heat, the tension building in every one of her nerve endings,; centring in a tight knot so he only had to brush her clitoris once and her body jerked.

She made a whimper of protest into his mouth when he removed his hand.

'Wait.' His hands smoothed away the tendrils of hair that had loosened from her pony-tail before framing her face to push her head back so he could look up into her eyes, searching, asking silent questions with each flicker of his thick lashes.

It felt as if he could see inside her.

Then, as if he'd found what he was looking for, his full mouth curled up at the corners, the blue of his eyes so dark and so deep that just looking into them made her poor battered heart ache, twist and shift in her chest all in one move. She shook her head, and smiled back.

'What?'

Gabe shrugged his shoulders, the tips of his thumbs smoothing back and forth against her flushed cheeks.

'Nothing.'

Ash laughed softly. 'I hate you *so* much.'

And Gabe smiled in reply. 'No, you don't.'

No, she didn't. Not any more. She almost wished she still did. Because hating him and losing him would be so much easier to survive than—

She closed her eyes and took a deep breath that crushed her breasts tighter against his chest. 'I will if you don't hurry up.'

Gabe rolled them over, the words vibrating against her mouth. 'I feel the sudden need to go *slowly*…'

And he did, for way too long, even when he was finally inside her—each deliberately slow slide of his hard length building the excruciating tension until she thought she would die from the need for release. Until she was clinging to the edge of sanity and pleading with him, the muscles in her thighs clenching, her breathing short and shallow, lips parting to gasp in the air filled with the undertones of his scent. And the words she didn't want to say were right there on the very tip of her tongue about to be said out loud…

But then wave after wave of intense pleasure rippled out over her body, Gabe's choking voice calling her name from what sounded like far away in the distance—so she swallowed the words back down, where they could wrap around her heart to keep it safe.

Because he might just have made love to her as if she was the woman he could continue to make love to for ever. But he hadn't denied that he thought they weren't going to last, *had he*?

CHAPTER TWELVE

''Cos you know this won't last.'

Gabe could still hear her voice saying the words. Trouble was they were completely at odds with the determined *'mine'* that was echoing deep inside him as he watched her from the edge of the room.

It was the old Pavlov's dog training gone ballistic.

He clenched his jaw as yet another man talking to her felt the need to touch her while he did. It wasn't much of a touch, none of them were: her hand held for a few seconds longer than it needed to be, fingers around her elbow to guide her to meet someone else, a palm to the small of her back as they leaned in to listen to what she was saying over the noise of the crowd. But every single touch earned a resounding and getting louder by the minute *'mine'* inside Gabe.

And he needed to get a handle on it before he ruined her opening-night party by feeling the need to thump someone. Now there was a way to tell the world.

She'd changed so much in the last eight years, hadn't she? And now that he knew this new version of her, the part of him that had sworn it would never look back and question his role in the train-wreck of their past had no choice but to open up the wound and examine it more closely. It'd been a hard decision to make.

He'd known exactly where she was since he'd arrived at the party—just late enough to blend into the crowd, his eyes seeking her out and skimming over the elegant lines of the green off-the-shoulder dress that moved just enough to hint at the curves of her as-close-to-perfect-as-be-damned body. The body he knew every inch of intimately and that merely looking at made him want to discover all over again.

Mine.

But watching her with hooded eyes from the periphery of the packed room as she worked the crowd with a smile constantly in place, her eyes shining bright as any jewels would if she'd worn them sparkling around her neck, on her wrist or dangling from her ears—not that she was wearing them or needed them to look better than she already did, he felt—he could see things he hadn't been able to see before.

Like the fact that her smile was a little too bright, her features a little too animated, her body language an exaggeration of her normal fluid movements—and he'd noticed all those things before he caught the number of times her hand would stray to that invisible strand that needed tucking away.

Polished, yes, beautiful without a doubt, but he'd lay odds she was as uncomfortable as hell underneath the sophistication she'd acquired with age and was doing everything she could not to let it show.

How come he'd never noticed before that she truly hated parties like these? Even when this one should have been one of the proudest moments of her life she was squirming inside, wasn't she? It made him think about the comments she'd made about being forced to attend them under the Fitzgerald name, about how people made veiled comments about her history right in front of her.

Why did she spend time with them? It kind of went against that fiercely independent streak of hers; the one that gave her the right to make choices—like telling them all to go to hell, for example. Yes, it was important the gallery made money, and that meant smiling at the kind of people who had money to spend. Gabe got that—he did a lot of smiling himself when it was called for; made for good business practice. But what Ash was doing was something else, wasn't it?

Her chin rose, her eyes skimming past the crowd and locking unerringly with his before she smiled a smaller, softer, more genuine smile that he answered with one of his own.

She'd been smiling that smile and making him smile back the way he was for quite some time, hadn't she?

Gabe couldn't remember ever feeling more of a sense of pride in another person as he did for what she'd done with her new project. She hadn't just risked everything financially, she'd made it a business that did good things along the way—like promoting struggling Irish artists and helping them add to the legacy of home-grown talent that'd gone before them, and giving space over rent-free to groups who used art to help people express themselves when they couldn't any other way, not to mention the money she had ploughed into her beloved Art Therapy programme.

That sense of pride made him stand a little taller even before he factored in how much bigger a guy he felt when her gaze would seek him out in the crowd, or how she would smile the way she just had when she found him, or how she would take a chance on being caught brushing her hand over his—or, in moments of daring, across his rear, on her way past.

Mine.

In time she found her way back across the room, eyes narrowing and chin lifting as she approached him with a gentle sway of her hips. 'You always do this, you know.'

'Do what?'

'Stand on the edge of these parties without mixing with the crowd.'

Fighting the automatic need to reach for her and remove any traces of another man's even innocent touch to restake his unspoken claim, he shrugged and glanced around the room. 'Old habits.'

When he looked back she had a thoughtful expression on her face, replaced in a heartbeat with a look of realization. 'You really have. I remember. Any time there were parties at the house when we were kids you used to hover in the doorways.'

Gabe took a deep breath and waited to see if she'd figure it out on her own. After all, with all the looking at the past he'd been doing of late he knew exactly why he did the things he did. It was an adult understanding, but back then he'd been a kid. And kids didn't rationalize or look to the future; they just felt what they felt.

She shook her head, as if telling him she thought he'd been wrong before she said aloud why he'd hovered in so many doorways at Fitzgerald parties.

'You thought you didn't belong there.' Her brows lifted as incredulity widened her eyes. 'You actually thought it wasn't your *place* to be there?'

Another deep breath created another shrug of his shoulders while he kept his voice purposefully calm. 'I wasn't one of you. I understood that from early on.'

Her long lashes flickered as she searched each of his eyes in turn, her voice dropping an octave. 'You were family to *me*.'

His mouth quirked. 'There was a line.'

'Since when?'

The husky question made him force his gaze away, because when she used that voice and looked at him like that the need to haul her in close was so strong it invoked a physical reaction—

kind of like a cramp across his chest. But answering questions was getting easier these days for both of them.

'You had those family pictures done every year. One year I asked my mother why we couldn't have our picture taken too. So she explained it to me in that very simplistic way you do with a little kid.'

'What did she say?'

'Doesn't matter any more.' He threw in a wink. 'I'm a big boy now.'

'I'd like to know.'

'Ash—'

'*Please.*' The word was said with a lift of her chin so he knew she was trying to hide behind bravado again before she added, 'We were gonna have to get round to attempting some of the more difficult stuff soon anyway, don't you think?'

'You wanna try some *now*?' He let out a short burst of laughter. She was kidding, right?

'In the middle of your party with all these nice people ready to throw money your way? *That's* when you think it's a good idea to wade into deeper water?'

His answer was a firm nod and the fold of her arms across her breasts. 'They've already spent enough money for me to go to bed happy tonight. Some of us were here earlier than other people. And we can't come to blows in public, can we? Any more than we can avoid the subject by doing something else; it's perfect. And it's just this one subject. Baby steps, Gabe.'

'And if I tell you the root cause of my habit of standing on the edges observing you'll tell me why it is you've never told anyone how much you hate being in the middle of it all, will you?'

Her breath caught. 'How can you possibly know—?'

He lifted his hand in front of his body, pointing his forefinger in the direction of his feet before he made a circling movement and leaned his head forwards to challenge her with raised eyebrows and a smile he knew she'd get. 'Over here in the land of observing the crowd, remember.'

With a purse of her lips and a roll of her eyes to indicate she still hated giving in he got, 'Okay, then.'

'Okay, you'll tell me if I tell you?'

'*You first.*'

For a man who'd spent years honing his negotiation skills so he always came out on the better end of a deal, he'd done a good job of not thinking about the small print, hadn't he?

As usual Ash wasn't done. 'But don't for one minute think that "doesn't matter any more" line washed with me. You're still always standing on the periphery, aren't you?'

'These days I'm confident enough in who and what I am to know that people will come to me—I don't have to go to them.' And as he said it he stood tall, so she knew he meant it.

'What did she say to you?'

He felt himself shrug again, as if he felt the need to shake the memories off now he was allowing himself to say them out loud. 'She said that it was a picture of the Fitzgeralds on their own because they were special and that we were different—we were a family of our own. A few weeks later she had your mother take some pictures of us and then every year she made sure when you lot had yours taken we had one done too. She still has them all framed and sat around the gatehouse on the estate; 'cos no matter how I try she won't quit working for your family.'

'What age were you when you asked?'

'Five or six.'

He'd said it all in a perfectly flat tone so she'd understand it was history and really didn't matter to him any more, but she still grimaced and felt the need to clear her throat before she spoke.

'And all you heard was that the Fitzgeralds were special and you were different from them, right? That's when you started developing the chip on your shoulder.'

'The one you knew to use against me, you mean?'

Oh, she disguised it well, and less than a few weeks ago he'd have missed it, but he saw the small flinch that indicated he'd hit a sore point. And he knew how far they'd come when she didn't fling something back in his face to fight hurt with hurt.

'Yes, but—'

Baby steps, she'd said, so that was enough of that one first time out, he felt.

'Now you tell me why you hate these things so much and why you're still doing so many of them when you do.'

The grimace was clearer, her need to look away from him and lift her hand to a stray curl that had actually loosened from her upswept hair enough to merit a tucking movement all adding together to tell the tale.

'I've hated these my whole life. Being a Fitzgerald never felt all that special to me.' She laughed, but the sound was brittle to his ears now he knew the sound of her laughter so well. 'If you look back you'll remember when I was little I used to stay in the doorway with you until it was my turn to be paraded before bed.'

'You used to try and hide behind me.' He could hear the edge of incredulity in his own voice. How had he forgotten that?

She threw him a warm smile. 'Yes, I did. And sometimes we managed to sneak away somewhere to play.'

'Until your father caught us that one time and made you come back in and meet people…'

'Yes.' The smile faded somewhat as she tilted her head towards her shoulder. 'My very first night being taught how to shake hands and meet people. He stood over me and gave me instructions for a good couple of hours.'

'Teaching you what a Fitzgerald was supposed to do.'

'Yes.'

'Smile brightly and shake hands with strangers and always say the right thing.'

'Hmm.' Her eyes softened at his understanding, the way they had more and more of late when she shared stuff with him and he pieced everything together. 'And let's face facts, that last one was always going to be the toughest one for me to get used to.'

Gabe rocked back a little, looking around the room while he let it all sink in. It shouldn't have been that big a surprise, not having watched it happening. But once again it came back to the fact he'd been watching through a child's eyes, hadn't he? A child didn't look at the bigger picture. But an adult could.

She'd been censored from an early age, been taught that her natural personality—the one full of fun, the need to laugh loud and often, and a tongue-in-cheek ability to say something just to tease that same laughter out of someone else—should be reined in for the sake of good manners in polite society.

They'd put her in some kind of goddamn gilded cage, hadn't they? Those *special* Fitzgeralds hadn't seen how amazing their daughter was in her own right. And she'd have to have felt that the real her was lacking somehow because of it, wouldn't she? Then compare her to Alex who had seemingly never been able to put a foot wrong.

He swore underneath his breath and mumbled, 'No wonder you started to rebel…'

'What?' Ash leaned a little closer to try and make out what he'd said.

But Gabe merely frowned as he asked the obvious question. 'So why are you letting yourself get roped into it all over again this time round? Because you're doing it, aren't you? You're putting on the face you think a Fitzgerald should at all these things you've been attending since the minute you got home, never letting anyone see the real you. Only this time you get hurt when they make assumptions based on your history. You're too smart not to know the one thing doesn't help the other. So why put yourself through it? Why not just be you and to hell with the ones that don't like it?'

He knew his voice was rising incrementally. But it made him angry—maybe even angrier than he had a right to be having judged her at face value for so long himself—but there was no need for her to do it any more, was there? She was a grown woman now, making her own way without financial assistance from the family, even when she could plainly have done with it.

She didn't owe anything to the name, except to be the Ashling Fitzgerald she really was—the Ash that he'd grown up with—the Ash who'd taken the tentative steps into womanhood before his very eyes—the Ash he'd always thought back then would one day—

But then she'd gone off the rails, proving to all those who thought she was unworthy of the Fitzgerald name that they were right—and then some.

If he hadn't kept pushing her the way he had when she'd come home he'd still believe that didn't-give-a-damn image was who she really was—and gone right ahead despising her for it. He'd have continued thinking she was lifting her pretty little nose in the air because she believed she was better than everyone else—the kind of person who could do whatever she wanted no matter what damage it did along the way. The spoilt little rich girl, rampaging around the country going wild, simply because she *could*—what did it matter? Who had the right to tell someone like her she couldn't do whatever the hell she liked?

When all that time she'd been lost and probably even a little angry, hadn't she? It'd been easier to let everyone believe what they did rather than try to prove them all wrong. And those special Fitzgeralds had sent her away when she'd shamed the name through no fault of her own, with pictures in the papers she hadn't even known had been taken of her.

While Gabe had actually had the gall to think she was beyond contempt for not appreciating how lucky she was. Had he been so determined that being born a Fitzgerald was the equivalent to owning the Holy Grail?

He was struggling hard to deal with the thoughts avalanching inside his head, and the very fact a *baby step* into the difficult years they'd been avoiding had rocked the convictions he'd held for over a decade, when she hit him with a blinder, her eyes scanning the room briefly as she spoke.

'I don't have a choice, not for a while anyway. It's part of the arrangement with my father. Once I've paid off my debt I can stop flying the Fitzgerald flag again and just be me, warts and all.'

'*What arrangement?*'

Ash blinked at him in stark astonishment. What the hell had brought on *that* reaction? He looked as if he were ready to kill someone with his bare hands!

She'd thought for a brief moment they stood a chance of breaking through into the difficult stuff with less bloodshed than might have been expected—barring the agony that went with knowing Gabe had felt at *five* that he was somehow less than everybody around him. That had hurt. As if his hurt were automatically hers now; wound him, she'd bleed. As it used to be once upon a time…

She took one look at the dark frown on his face, his jaw so tense she thought he might even be grinding his teeth again— and it brought on the urgent need to glance around them to see if anyone else was seeing it.

Gabe stepped in, towering over her until she looked up into his eyes. '*What* arrangement?'

What exactly was his problem?

'Would you calm down?' She widened her eyes so he knew she was serious. 'I don't see how—'

The burst of laughter was anything but amused, his fingers wrapping around her upper arm to turn her in the direction of the door below the stairs. 'If the next words involve you saying it's not any of my business, then you can forget it.'

Ash was torn between letting herself get angry at his behaviour and trying to calm him down so he didn't make a scene, clenching her own teeth to stage-whisper up at him, 'Where exactly do you think you're taking me? I'm the hostess, for crying out loud!'

He stopped dead. 'You prefer we do this here?'

'I don't know what *this* is!' She attempted yanking her arm free when they were out of view, only to have his hold tighten. 'Gabe, stop it—you're *hurting* me.'

He frowned looking down at her arm, as if he'd not quite realized what he was doing, the hold loosening and his thumb brushing her skin as if to try and make it better. Then his gaze rose, his deep voice dropping to a low, deathly calm. 'I need to know what kind of arrangement he forced you into. Then we're getting you the hell out of it so he never interferes in either of our lives ever again.'

'*Either* of our lives?'

With a swift glance to make sure no one was under the stairs with them, Gabe lowered his head. 'You think you're the first, do you?'

Ash stepped back, swaying on her heels as she stared at him with wide eyes and an open mouth. *What?* And her face must have said a thousand words, because Gabe let go of her arm,

turning his face away, a muscle in his jaw jumping before he
glanced sideways at her from beneath hooded eyes.

'Welcome to the club.'

There was no way in hell she wasn't following him out the
door after that.

'*What did he make you do?*'

And her stomach literally lurched when she saw the look on
his face as he turned. Whatever it had been had been a really
big deal to Gabe, hadn't it? So big that it had been kept a secret
for how long?

It cost more than she thought she had in her to keep her voice
calm. 'When was this?'

Gabe swore and began pacing up and down in front of her,
stopping suddenly to drop his head back and look at the night
sky as he took a breath. 'I was fifteen.'

Fifteen? 'What did you need the money for?'

He dropped his chin and looked her straight in the eye. 'I
didn't go looking for it, if that's what you mean. He approached
me.'

'To offer to pay for *what*?' The energy required to keep her
voice calm was rapidly getting used up. She'd known her father
was a difficult man to deal with—hell, she of *all people* knew—
but to have tried to manipulate Gabe at fifteen to get what he
wanted—

It was beyond stooping low.

Gabe had gone entirely too calm for her liking. 'School.'

Ash felt a pain so sharp in her chest it literally made her
catch her breath. Of course. Gabe's mother had so wanted for
him to have a good education—had sat on him to make sure he
got good marks in his exams, as any mother would. And Gabe
had always been smart. It had just never occurred to Ash back
then how he'd been able to switch to the same top-notch school
as her brother.

She bent forwards, lifting her hands to her hips while she tried to catch her breath. Her father had paid for it. But rather than just doing the right thing and paying for it simply because he could—he'd had to make some kind of an arrangement with Gabe. So that Gabe, who already had a chip on his shoulder, was forced to swallow his pride in order to get the best start he could in life.

Gulping in deep breaths of air, Ash tried hard to absorb some of the sheer agony into her body. Hurt Gabe; she'd bleed. And right now, she was bleeding.

When she looked up from beneath her lashes she found him standing every inch of his six three tall—as if he felt he had to. And it killed her, because he didn't have to, not with her—*never with her*. He was five hundred times the man the supposedly great Arthur Fitzgerald was in her eyes. Didn't he know that?

She forced herself upright. 'You opted out of going to university to pay it off quicker, didn't you?'

'Yes.'

'With interest, I'll bet.'

'Yes.'

She nodded. 'And made sure he knew he'd never get a chance to own you ever again, right?'

'I believe I used the phrase "rot in hell before I ever need your help again".' He smirked, the blue of his eyes icy, as if he could see her father in front of him. 'I might have thrown an "old bastard like you" in somewhere for good measure.'

'I'm very glad to hear it.' And she was, not to mention incredibly proud of him for standing up to the older man. He really was amazing, wasn't he?

When she smiled at him he stared at her for a long time; she couldn't even see him blinking. And that was when she knew— she knew he was waiting for her to ask the obvious. And, Lord help her, she didn't want to ask.

She shivered, hard, tears threatening in the backs of her eyes. Because she already knew, didn't she? With Gabe's fierce pride, even at that age, there'd have been only the one thing her father could have used to get him to agree to borrowing money: emotional blackmail.

Her voice crackled on the words. 'What did he ask you to do, Gabe?'

She could see it in his eyes without him saying it. And now she was bleeding from every pore.

'He made you my keeper, didn't he?' She nodded because she didn't need him to confirm it; she already knew. 'I was already starting to dig my heels in by then and he knew he couldn't control me for ever so he made sure he had you on the payroll years before I went off the rails. He used the fact that we were close—'

Her voice broke on the words, forcing her to stop and take more deep breaths. Every time he'd been there. Every single time she'd been stuck somewhere and didn't want her parents to know so she'd called Gabe to come get her. Every time she'd gone to a party that had got out of hand and he'd swooped in to rescue her…

She'd thought Gabe had been there because he was the one person who cared enough to always be there, no matter what she did. It was why that last day had hurt so much—when he'd kissed her and she'd known in that moment she'd lost the only person who still mattered, the one person who kept her grounded. And all that time he'd been there, not because he cared, but because he'd been paid to be there.

Because how could he possibly have continued caring when she was a constant reminder of his debt to the Fitzgeralds? He had to have started hating her then. If she hadn't been so rebellious, if she'd toed the line and managed to be what her father wanted her to be—

Her father had used the fact Gabe cared about her to make it not just a 'business arrangement' with him, but a betrayal of her if he turned it down—that was how Gabe would have seen it, wasn't it? That was exactly how *her Gabe* would have seen it. He'd have thought by sacrificing his pride he'd be helping protect her from her father somehow...

Now it all made sense. It wasn't just that she'd humiliated him that day; she'd reminded him he'd had to sell his soul because he was the housekeeper's son. The housekeeper's son who dared to get close to Princess Fitzgerald only to have her high-and-mighty-ness hit his weakness to save face in front of her posh friends.

No wonder he'd hated her as much as he had for as long as he had. And how could he ever care for her again when he'd gone through all that because of her?

Goose-bumps, nothing to do with the temperature, broke out on her arms so she lifted her hands and rubbed them away while she stared at a point in the middle of Gabe's broad chest.

He took a step forwards; she took a step back.

What was she supposed to do with this information? Was she supposed to hate him for letting her father force him into it? She couldn't do that—he'd been fifteen, for crying out loud. Was she supposed to hate him for not telling her? If he had she'd have gone crazy sooner, wouldn't she? And mightn't have had enough maturity on the flipside to pull herself together when things got as bad as they had.

Gabe tried another step forwards; she took another step back and managed to look up at him, her voice just above a whisper.

'*Don't.*' She didn't want to think it was the same kind of plea it had become of late, so she reinforced the word with a shake of her head. 'Please don't.'

His deep voice was husky when he spoke. 'I'll pay off whatever you owe him so this can stop once and for all. No more running around flying the Fitzgerald flag for that manipulative old bastard, you hear me?'

No. She shook her head, not quite sure if she'd said it out loud or not. 'It's just putting me in debt to you then. And we have enough problems, don't we?'

'I can promise you it'd be proviso-free, Ash.'

She shook her head; it seemed to be all she could do, 'I can't, Gabe.'

'Then get Alex to pay it off. He won't hold it over you either—you should have gone to him in the first place. Why didn't you?' His voice, still husky, held an edge of frustration to it.

And Ash needed him to understand so she let it all spill out in a flat matter-of-fact tine. 'I thought if I dealt with my father he could see I was prepared to face up to the consequences of my actions. I guess I felt I owed him that after all the humiliation I brought the family name. I wouldn't take money when they sent me to France, you see, 'cos I knew then I had to grow up and I wanted to make it on my own. When the money I saved wasn't enough to open the gallery he offered to pay for all of it, but I couldn't do that either, not without a repayment plan. And that meant negotiating with him. Smiling the Fitzgerald smile didn't seem that high a price to pay at the time.'

But that'd been before she'd known all this.

She saw his chest rise and fall with another deep breath, his voice calmer again. 'Promise me you'll talk to Alex.'

Finally she managed a nod.

'Good.'

Turning on her heel she started back to the door, unable to understand why she was so damn calm on the outside when inside she was bleeding to death.

Then, hand on the door, she turned and looked over her shoulder at Gabe where he was standing watching her every move. She let her gaze move up from the safe point in the centre of his chest, past the V of his open shirt collar, up the column of his neck, lingering on his mouth for a little until she summoned the strength to look into the deep blue of his eyes.

She ached more than she'd ever ached. 'I might need a while with this.'

He frowned at the softly spoken words. 'How long?'

'A while.' She shrugged the shoulder she was looking over, tried a smile but couldn't get it to work properly. 'It's a lot, Gabe.'

'I don't know how long I can give you.'

Well, she couldn't really blame him if he moved on, could she? Not now she knew it all.

'Guess you were right about keeping it all secret, weren't you? Us, I mean.' She didn't want him to think she blamed him for the other secret he'd carried. 'I can see the problems we might've encountered if we'd gone public. My father might even have used it to split us up…'

'He could've tried.'

She nodded, turning back to the door.

'Don't take too long, Ash.'

'I won't.' But she knew it was a lie. She was going to have to put some distance between them now, wasn't she? 'Cos even if they'd managed to work their way through everything else, there was just no way around this one, was there? It was the proverbial pink elephant in the room that nobody wanted to mention.

Ash was gonna have to let him go.

CHAPTER THIRTEEN

FRANKLY Gabe didn't know how much more time he could give Ash. But he'd taken one look at her face when she'd pieced just some of it together and immediately known telling her the rest might be one push too many when she was already so close to the edge. And he damn well wasn't letting it happen twice in his lifetime.

But she needn't bother trying to run this time either. Wherever she went, he'd find her.

To occupy mind and body, he joined crews wherever they were a man short, just like the early days. Work had been his escape last time too, hadn't it? And it was amazing how therapeutic knocking down walls with a sledgehammer was, not to mention the hours of amusement to be had when some of the workers realized who it was swinging it beside them.

He was a million miles away from the boy who'd made the deal that'd ultimately led him to where he was now, with younger men upping their efforts just because the boss was there. And yet he was no different from that boy deep down, was he? Because he still wanted the one thing more than anything else, didn't he?

Not that he'd have confessed it with his dying breath if it'd been tortured out of him less than six weeks ago. Hell, no, he'd even done a good job of convincing himself it hadn't been real, hadn't he?

That he was over her.

Well, there was no arguing it now, probably hadn't been since the night he'd found her crying in his garden. Last time he hadn't been patient enough to work at it, that was all. Not that he was any less *impatient* now, but he could damn well make himself learn to be patient if that was what it took. Hadn't he already demonstrated his patience by keeping their relationship a secret for as long as he had?

And he'd given her almost a week now. That showed patience, right? Mind you, one more day and that was it. Now he'd had so much time to think things through, he had a better plan.

A plan that went straight to hell when he opened a newspaper at lunchtime to find her face smiling up at him from a photograph above the boldly printed:

FITZGERALD FAMILY GATHER TO HONOUR FAMOUS FATHER.

One last day of smiling for the masses and she was done; *no more*. And even if she hadn't had the knock-down shouting match she had with her father to tell him as much, there was just no way she could continue to smile sweetly for guests at future parties in the house while surrounded by constant reminders of her long history with Gabe.

To add to the agony there was then the fact that both their mothers seemed hell-bent on telling every Gabe and Ash story they could remember from the annals of all time while they'd all had afternoon tea before the cocktail party officially began.

And as fascinating as it was to her that the two women seemed to have as close a relationship as Gabe and Alex did—somehow balancing something right against all that had been so very wrong—it still took a gargantuan effort to smile her way through it.

She missed him so bad it felt as if she'd had a limb removed, and that was after a week. How bad would it feel in two weeks, or three, or in a month? Because she knew it wasn't going to get better with time. Not now she'd been with him the way she had: watching the beginning of a slow smile when she woke up beside him; listening to the laughter she loved best when she'd learned how to tease it out of him; sitting on a sofa with him talking for hours and then kissing for twice as long as that; knowing what it was like having him inside her body as she fell apart at the seams...

She missed him *so-o-o much.*

But she'd get through this last party if it killed her. And then she could go back to her place and try to formulate a way to get on with the rest of her life.

'Gabriel Burke—'

She blinked in confusion when she thought she heard his name whispered in the crowd, shaking her head at her foolishness. It was just his name was constantly in her mind, so naturally she now thought she could hear it in the damn wind as well.

'Security wouldn't let him...I think Alex...'

Great, she was losing her mind. Looking around the crowd peppered with famous faces, Ireland's elite come to pay its respects to her father's latest award, she attempted to locate where the snippets of conversation were coming from. Before the nice men in white coats appeared to fit her with a straitjacket...

'...construction—B.D.L.—Signs all over Dublin.'

Now *that* she definitely *had* heard, so she turned to find out who was risking life and limb by taking his name in vain within earshot of her. Only to stare in amazement as, almost in slow motion, the crowd parted like the Red Sea to reveal Gabe striding towards her with a look of sheer determination on his face, his eyes fixed on her and only her.

Ash forgot how to breathe.

She took in his workmanlike clothes: well-worn jeans stained with grey dust and a T-shirt that'd probably been white before he started work that morning. She watched the breeze toss his unruly hair into his eyes, she saw the muscles in his forearms flex as he clenched his large hands into fists at his sides. And she was so lost in all those sights that she didn't even look around at the sea of people in their vastly contrasting cocktail dresses and pristine suits to see who else was watching him marching her way.

She didn't care who was watching. *Gabe was there.*

When he shot a dangerous look to her left she glanced over and found her father, standing with folded arms, watching. But she didn't give him a chance to make a comment, her feet immediately carrying her forwards.

Lifting her brows in question, she leaned her upper body towards him when he got close, her voice low.

'*What are you doing?*'

Gabe shrugged his broad shoulders. 'I warned you not to take too long, didn't I?'

But she'd thought he meant—

Before she could answer he bent over and swept her off her feet, turning on his heel to walk back in the same direction he'd come from. While Ash stared at his profile in stark amazement.

'Done with the secret bit then, I take it?'

'Yes, we are.'

Was it very wrong of her to ignore the stern tone to his voice and forget every problem in favour of giving into the bubbling, ridiculously joyful happiness she felt because of that? Ash didn't think so, but she left it inside to be on the safe side, linking her hands behind his neck and letting her fingers feel the tips of the hair she loved so much, her eyes taking in every detail of his familiar features. *Lord, how she'd missed him.*

'What brought this on?'

'It was happening tomorrow but your face in the paper moved it up a day.'

Ash's heart was beating a salsa. 'I don't actually have a party for you to carry me out of tomorrow.'

'Well, then, it's as well I came to claim you today, isn't it?'

He'd come to—

She blinked at him with wide eyes, convinced any second she might wake up. 'Claim me?'

'Yup.'

'So—I'm *yours* now, am I?'

He stopped walking at the edge of the house, turning his face to look straight into her eyes before informing her in a deep rumble, 'Ash, you were mine from the day your mother brought you home as a baby.'

All those Gabe and Ash stories their mothers had told from the annals of all time? Had she missed…?

'*Oh.*'

The edges of his mouth quirked when she couldn't think of anything else to say, then he started walking again; gaze focussed forwards on wherever it was he was taking her to. And much as she'd love to give into the idea of twittering birds and a sunset to walk into, Ash couldn't stay silent for long, not while things still weren't clear in her head.

'Correct me if I'm wrong, but 'til as recently as Friday night you didn't want anyone to know we were sleeping together; you didn't think we'd last.'

'No, you *told* me that's what I thought.'

'You didn't disagree with me.'

He shot her a frown. 'I *showed* you you were wrong.'

By making love to her the way he had? And she was supposed to have known that *how* exactly?

She heard gravel crunch beneath his feet. 'You still didn't want anyone to know about us.'

'We needed time on our own first. I reckoned if we managed to build a strong enough foundation we stood a better chance of surviving the outside world. And you'd burned me once already—you honestly think I was letting that happen in front of an audience again?'

Why hadn't she thought about the second part of that? The first part would never have occurred to her, because it meant he'd actually thought about—

He stopped and looked around him, almost as if he needed to get his bearings before he moved again—off the gravel and down the rolling bank in front of the house—marching them towards the tree line. And while his words rattled around inside her head Ash tore her eyes from his face long enough to try and see where they were going, her heart twisting painfully when she knew—because he was taking her back to where it had started.

So she stayed silent until he sat down on the old swing, the ropes creaking in protest while he settled her across his hard lap. Then, one at a time, he moved his arms so he had the ropes secured inside his elbows, before holding her close again, his voice low and even.

'I wanted to kill him, you know.'

'Wanted to kill who?'

'Miles.'

Who? She had no idea what he was talking about, and she already felt as if she'd fallen down the rabbit hole in Alice's story. But Gabe cleared things up for her, continuing in a low voice while his fingers played with the material of her dress at her waist.

'When I went looking for you that night and found him plastered all over you I saw red. He was lucky I didn't rip his damn head off. So when you tried telling me you thought you were in love with him it didn't exactly help—I'd probably have kissed you even if you hadn't goaded me into it.'

Ash studied his face while he allowed the swing to sway them a little, her eyes taking in the familiar features she loved so much with a brand-new understanding forming in her brain. But she was afraid to say it, was afraid to even let herself think it in case she was wrong.

'You had to have hated me for what my father forced you into…'

He looked surprised by that, dark brows folding above his eyes. 'Why would I hate you for that? You had nothing to do with it. And I'd have tried to keep you outta trouble even if he hadn't made that arrangement with me—you just didn't make it easy for me, and that meant I got to have regular lectures from the old man about how I wasn't living up to my end of the deal.'

She cringed, inside and out. 'But if you hadn't cared about me he'd never have been able to get you to accept that money to begin with.'

'Oh I'm sure he'd have tried something else.'

'But if you hadn't—'

'Loved you?'

The question was asked with a small smile on his mouth and the blue in his eyes clouded with enough tenderness to make her vision blur.

He moved a hand to tuck her hair behind her ear. 'You keep using the word "cared"—let's be brave and have a go at the "L" word, shall we?'

'I knew you loved me.' Her voice shook on the words, 'You were the best friend I had, Gabe—the only one who took the time to yell at me when I did things to try and get attention. And I loved you for that.'

'Until I crossed the line and kissed you.'

'And made me feel a hundred different things I wasn't anywhere near ready to feel. I hated you for that, because I lost my best friend that day.'

'So you said things to hurt me as much as I'd hurt you.' He trapped the lock of hair he'd tucked away between his thumb and forefinger, watching as he trailed down its length to skim her breast. 'I get it now. But at the time all I knew was how much I loved you—and not just in a best friends kind of way; that changed a while before that night.'

He'd been *in love* with her?

The moan of agony started at the pit of her stomach as the full impact of it set in. No matter what new information she got to make her look at that night again with fresh eyes, it all kept coming back to the one thing: her Gabe had been hurt deeply. And now she was bleeding again. When the moan escaped her lips she moved her hands, sliding her arms tighter round the thick column of his neck as she leaned her forehead against his jaw.

'I didn't know.'

'You weren't s'posed to know.'

'You could have told me.'

'You weren't ready to hear it.'

He was right. But, oh, how much she ached knowing he'd felt that way and she'd rejected him the way she had. 'I'm sorry, Gabe—I really am.'

She felt him press a kiss against her hair. 'It's all right—we're fixing it now. We just needed a second run at it, that's all.'

Ash breathed deep, filling her senses with his scent as if re-assuring herself he was really there and it was going to be all right after all, when she'd been mentally preparing herself to let him go. Emotion welling up inside her like a tidal wave as she allowed herself to fully understand what she'd have lost by not taking a chance the way he had by coming to claim her, she turned her face into the crook of his neck and said the words against his skin.

'I love you so much.' How could she not?

He moved his head back a little. 'I didn't quite catch that—you might need to say it a little louder.'

When she lifted her head and looked up at him she saw the sparkle in his eyes. Oh, he'd heard her all right, but if he needed to be told a few million times then she didn't have a problem with that.

'I *love* you. I knew I was falling in love with you the night you sent me to the stupid spare room. Not being able to shout it to the world this last while has *killed* me—why do you think I was pushing so hard?'

Eyes still sparkling, he quirked his brows at her, his arms briefly tightening. 'You could possibly have tried telling *me* first.'

Ash nodded, smiling at him the way she'd wanted to smile at him for weeks. 'I could. But I wasn't sure you were ready to hear it.'

'I was ready.'

Stilling the swaying of the swing with his feet, he wrapped his arms so tight around her she could barely breathe, lowering his mouth to hers to steal away what little air she had left in her lungs with a fierce kiss filled with hunger. And Ash fed that hunger with every ounce of the passion the mere thought of him had aroused in her from her first night home, moving her arms so her fingers could thread into his unruly hair.

They kissed for ever, taking and giving until the hunger could only be satisfied one other way, a low growl of frustration sounding in the base of Gabe's throat as he tore his lips free, resting his forehead against hers, his eyes opening to look deep into hers while he told her, 'Even when I was determined to despise you I wanted you, Ash—it was part of the reason I hated you so much. I didn't want to love you this time round, did a good job of blocking it out from the first time as it happens, but I don't think I ever stopped. Out of sight out of mind helped, mind you. But once you came home that was that. You're mine.' His arms squeezed in warning. '*Say it.* Say it so I know you get it this time.'

Ash sobbed, just the once, laughed and then swore softly. 'I hate you for making me cry. I hate crying.'

He smiled when she sniffed loudly. 'If it helps any, it's not easy to watch either. Now say it.'

'Yes, I'm yours, you idiot.' Untangling her fingers, she framed his gorgeous face and moved it back so she could let him see the sincerity in her eyes. 'I told my father today that I'd happily carry your name for the rest of my days rather than try to be a Fitzgerald like him. And I meant it, Gabe—even though I thought I was going to lose you again.'

'You're not gonna lose me and, for the record—' he moved forward to press another kiss against her lips, his large hands smoothing up and down against her back '—if I didn't already love you as much as I do, I'd love you for having the guts to say that to his face. I'll just bet he was chuffed to bits at the idea of you marrying the housekeeper's son.'

'If I do it won't be to spite him—it'll be because *I love you.*'

Gabe's mouth quirked, then developed into a full-blown dimpled smile. 'What do you mean "if"? That kinda implies you get a choice in the matter.'

Ash rolled her eyes. 'There you go bossing me around again. You know how I feel about my independence...'

'Tough.' With a punishing kiss to tell her there was no point in arguing, he unwrapped his arms from the ropes and pushed up onto his feet, tossing her up into a more secure position before he started marching back towards the house. 'And now I'm gonna take you home and spend the entire weekend persuading you there's no reason you can't keep your independence and still be married to me at the same time. I want the entire world to understand you're mine.'

'I think they got the message with the whole *Officer and a Gentleman* thing you just did.' When he threw a look of amused confusion down at her she laughed, the bubbling, ridiculously joyful happiness she felt just too large to contain any longer. 'It's a film.'

'It's a girl's film, isn't it?'

'Yes, it is.' Letting her feet swing back and forth, she tilted her head round to look up into his eyes, cupping her palm against his cheek and touching her thumb to the edge of his mouth. 'Not that I'm not completely and utterly in favour of the method of persuasion you have in mind for the weekend—but, just so you know, my answer's already "yes". And that might seem quick for some people, but we've already wasted too much time haven't we? So whenever, wherever, it's yes.'

Gabe turned his head and pressed his lips to her palm before smiling the kind of purely sexual smile that sent shivers of anticipation up her spine. 'Still gonna have to persuade you, though...'

She smiled when he bent his head to place his mouth just above her ear. ''Cos there's more. And I'm thinking if I make love to you until you can't move then you won't have a problem with getting married as soon as humanly possible. I'm thinking a couple of weeks from now—less if we can manage it.'

Ash looked up at him with wide eyes. '*Gabe*—are you telling me you're pregnant? I thought we were careful. We were careful lots and lots.'

He laughed the kind of laugh she loved so much, his arms

squeezing her against his chest again. 'I can guarantee you I'm not pregnant.'

'Then what's the rush? You've got me—I promise—I'm yours and I honestly couldn't love you any more than I already do.'

'Well, so long as you remember I loved you first.' He stopped beside his truck, kissing her long and slow before grinning at her. 'We're not doing it to spite your father, Ash—but you gotta admit: being in love, getting married and living the rest of our days together is one hell of a way of getting even.'

'I love the way your mind works sometimes, you know.' It occurred to her that he maybe hadn't thought about the fact he was about to get Arthur Fitzgerald as his father-in-law, but still. 'Tell you what—take me home and persuade me some—and we'll see…'

Gabe took a deep breath, setting her back on her feet and claiming her lips in the kind of kiss that made her ache all over. 'You know the chances of your father giving away the bride to me are slim, don't you?'

Looping her thumbs into the belt loops of his jeans, Ash leaned forwards onto her tiptoes, her chin lifting. 'That's his choice. If he cares at all about me being happy then he'll have to understand *you* make me happy. And, anyway, I have a sneaking suspicion our mothers will be over the moon.'

'Well, then, the old man gets to be the odd one out—' he set his hands on her hips, fingers playing before he drew her in against him, his mouth hovering over hers '—'cos that brother of yours got me past the security here with a pat on the back and somethin' that sounded like "about time too".'

Ash smiled against his lips. 'Don't you just hate it when he's right?'

'Not this time, I don't.' He brushed her mouth with his, once, twice, his eyes still focused on hers. 'Say it again.'

He didn't need to tell her what he meant. 'I'm yours, Gabe. I always will be. I love you.'

'Love you too.'

Ash whispered the words against his mouth with a smile on her lips and her heart in her eyes:

'My Gabe.'

His eyes sparkled down at her. 'Now you're home.'

HARLEQUIN *Presents*

Demure but defiant...
Can three international playboys
tame their disobedient brides?

Lynne Graham

presents

Virgin **BRIDES** ♥ Arrogant **HUSBANDS**

Proud, masculine and passionate, these men are used
to having it all. In stories filled with drama, desire
and secrets of the past, find out how these arrogant
husbands capture their hearts.

THE GREEK TYCOON'S DISOBEDIENT BRIDE
Available December 2008, Book #2779

THE RUTHLESS MAGNATE'S VIRGIN MISTRESS
Available January 2009, Book #2787

THE SPANISH BILLIONAIRE'S PREGNANT WIFE
Available February 2009, Book #2795

HP12787

HARLEQUIN *Presents*

EXTRA

HIRED: FOR THE BOSS'S PLEASURE

She's gone from personal assistant
to mistress—but now he's demanding
she become the boss's bride!

Read all our fabulous stories this month:

MISTRESS: HIRED FOR THE BILLIONAIRE'S PLEASURE
by INDIA GREY

THE BILLIONAIRE BOSS'S INNOCENT BRIDE
by LINDSAY ARMSTRONG

HER RUTHLESS ITALIAN BOSS
by CHRISTINA HOLLIS

MEDITERRANEAN BOSS, CONVENIENT MISTRESS
by KATHRYN ROSS

REQUEST YOUR FREE BOOKS!

 HARLEQUIN *Presents* ®

2 FREE NOVELS PLUS 2 FREE GIFTS!

YES! Please send me 2 FREE Harlequin Presents® novels and my 2 FREE gifts (gifts are worth about $10). After receiving them, if I don't wish to receive any more books, I can return the shipping statement marked "cancel". If I don't cancel, I will receive 6 brand-new novels every month and be billed just $4.05 per book in the U.S. or $4.74 per book in Canada, plus 25¢ shipping and handling per book and applicable taxes, if any*. That's a savings of close to 15% off the cover price! I understand that accepting the 2 free books and gifts places me under no obligation to buy anything. I can always return a shipment and cancel at any time. Even if I never buy another book, the two free books and gifts are mine to keep forever.

106 HDN ERRW   306 HDN ERRL

Name	(PLEASE PRINT)	
Address		Apt. #
City	State/Prov.	Zip/Postal Code

Signature (If under 18, a parent or guardian must sign)

Mail to the Harlequin Reader Service:
IN U.S.A.: P.O. Box 1867, Buffalo, NY 14240-1867
IN CANADA: P.O. Box 609, Fort Erie, Ontario L2A 5X3

Not valid to current subscribers of Harlequin Presents books.

Want to try two free books from another line?
Call 1-800-873-8635 or visit www.morefreebooks.com.

* Terms and prices subject to change without notice. N.Y. residents add applicable sales tax. Canadian residents will be charged applicable provincial taxes and GST. Offer not valid in Quebec. This offer is limited to one order per household. All orders subject to approval. Credit or debit balances in a customer's account(s) may be offset by any other outstanding balance owed by or to the customer. Please allow 4 to 6 weeks for delivery. Offer available while quantities last.

Your Privacy: Harlequin Books is committed to protecting your privacy. Our Privacy Policy is available online at www.eHarlequin.com or upon request from the Reader Service. From time to time we make our lists of customers available to reputable third parties who may have a product or service of interest to you. If you would prefer we not share your name and address, please check here. ☐

HP08R

HARLEQUIN *Presents*

kept for his
Pleasure

She's his mistress on demand!

Wherever seduction takes place, these fabulously
wealthy, charismatic, sexy men know how to
keep a woman coming back for more!

She's his mistress on demand—but when he
wants her body *and soul* he will be demanding
a whole lot more! Dare we say it…even marriage!

CONFESSIONS OF A
MILLIONAIRE'S MISTRESS
by Robyn Grady

**Don't miss any books in
this exciting new miniseries
from Harlequin Presents!**

www.eHarlequin.com

HP12801